THE
MEDICAL
PROJECT

Nicholas Licausi

ISBN: 979-8-88615-224-1 (Paperback)

Inks and Bindings
888-290-5218
www.inksandbindings.com
orders@inksandbindings.com

Contents

Dedication

This book is dedicated to my wife, our daughter, and son.

I like nice endings but, in real life, this does not always happen.

After a long struggle, our daughter died of cancer. I feel this could have been prevented, and many other deaths. If the world could make better use of technology and had more focus on how to find cures for diseases

This book is one of the series of books that will be written that is fictional but also has some solutions to problems in the world today. It will show a way of improving our health, around the world, by using technology. Hopefully, it will be read by someone with power that can get a project like this started in the United States.

Foreword

I am not a writer and have not had the time to sit down and write a book. After my daughter's death, I wrote this book to get my mind off the pain my wife and I was experiencing.

Even though the book is fictional, there are many ideas in it that, if implemented, could solve many medical problems in our society today. I have tried to make the book fun to read and even wrote it with the idea that if someone wanted to make it into a movie, it could be done.

When writing, the ideas flowed quickly onto the paper. Also, as I wrote, it seemed like I was there, and it was like watching a movie. I tried to write the book in plain English so it would be easy for all people to read.

All of the content in the book was written by me. I did not have a ghostwriter or co-writer. In fact, the hardest thing for me was the editing which I did get help from others. I enjoyed doing this book so much. I have started another book, and as this one focuses on the Medical Industry and things that can be done to improve that industry, the next book will focus on a different industry.

Acknowledgment

I would like to thank Rosemary Morgan, Henry Prior, Karen Johnson Prior and Susan Hess Krisman for all helping me get through a horrible time I went through after my wife's death. They all had an interest in my book and Susie and Karen helped with editing.

I would also like to thank Lorie Jones and her team for their work on the book.

Additionally, Jim Addison's work in marketing the book was outstanding which gave me incentive to start two more books.

MEETING AT LODGE AND WHITE HOUSE

It was a cool, clear Friday morning in the West Virginia Mountains. This was the first vacation John and Kate Colombo had been able to take in three years, and they only could be away for four days. They decided to take it at a lodge on the Cheat River just a few miles from where they graduated from college.

The lodge they were staying at was over sixty years old and built of bricks and logs with a vast porch in front. The Cheat River flowed rapidly along one side of the hotel, and the mountains were on the other side. When you walked into the hotel, there was a grand lobby area with a fireplace and, off to one side, a large dining area. John and Kate had a room upstairs facing the river and were staying at the hotel for the weekend and checked in on Thursday.

John is notably tall and handsome in an approachable, eccentric, and gruff manner. He's athletic and strong while simultaneously appearing slim and rangy. His hazel eyes and brown hair have gone silver-grey with time. Many people would mistake John for Harrison Ford. Not only in how he looked but also in how he acted.

Meanwhile, Kate had black hair, and brown eyes. She looked a little like Sandra Bullock. Both were in their late forties and very fit. Kate and John met when Kate was in her last year of high school, and John was in his first year of college and married four years later.

A few years after they married, they had a baby girl. After their daughter graduated from college, she got a job and moved to her apartment. When she moved out of the house, it was like dating again. They would spend time going to the movies and out for dinner.

Everything changed a year ago when their daughter got cancer. The project they were both working on with the State Department for two years was suddenly terminated. When Kate and John were told the project was terminated, they then decided to go on a leave of absence so they could focus on taking care of their daughter.

Between work and taking care of their daughter, they have not been able to take a vacation in several years. Their daughter was feeling better, so they decided they could go on this short vacation. On this vacation, they just wanted to relax and relieve some stress.

It was Saturday morning, and they had just woken up. Even when they are on vacation, they would still wake up at seven. John was out of bed looking out the window at the Cheat River, and Kate was in bed looking at the TV. They were both in their PJs.

John smiled at Kate and said, "You know I love you. What do you think about having breakfast and then heading out for a run? After that, can we go shopping? There is a running path that stretches along the river."

Kate looked up and smiled at John and said, "I love you, John. I will skip the run but will have breakfast and do some shopping. What are you going to wear for breakfast?"

"I think I will wear my running clothes. What about you?"

Kate looked at John with that same smile and said, "I guess I will wear my shopping clothes."

John then said, "I will wear my shopping-clothes when I shop with you."

They are both fit and do some exercise, whether it is yoga, swimming, or running.

John tries to run every day, and Kate runs about three times per week.

They got dressed, brushed their teeth, opened the door to their room, proceeded down the hall, and then down the stairs to the lobby.

There was a restaurant with a view of the Cheat River just off the lobby, where they served all the meals. There is limited seating in this restaurant, so when Kate and John walked in, they were seated across from an older gentleman.

Being seated with other people at your table is often done in this restaurant and some European restaurants. Kate and John were used to this way of seating since they have done a great deal of travel.

The gentleman looked like he was about 65 years old. He looked exhausted, and you could tell he had worked in the coal mines of West Virginia because no matter how hard coal miners try, they never seem to be able to get all the coal dust out of their skin.

In this restaurant, everyone gets coffee, toast, cereal, and eggs. It is served country style where everything is already on the table. The older gentleman then lifted the coffee, which was close to him, and motioned to Kate and John with the pot, saying, "Would you like a cup of coffee. Let me introduce myself. I am Joe Christopher. How often do you come to West Virginia?"

John answered, "It has been about ten years since we were here last. We do not come back to West Virginia enough. It is a place where the countryside is so relaxing, and the people are really nice. It is a place where people bake you pies, lend you furniture, and when they know you are in need, they always help. It is a place where you never hear about murder, rape, or stealing. It is a shame, but since there is very little business in the State, it is a place where people must leave in order to get work. Do you live in West Virginia?"

"Yes, I was born here and still live here. I am picking up some relatives at the hotel. I know you are right about what you said; people get their degrees and leave. My daughter Diane went to West Virginia University and got her degree. As soon as she got her degree, she left West Virginia. I can't blame her. She got a fantastic job. She's been able to travel to France, Spain, Italy, Tokyo, and other places around the world. She even did some modeling. She is coming home today."

John and Kate could relate to Joe. His daughter sounded almost like their daughter. They could tell when he talked that he was serious about what he was saying, and he also had a somber look on his face. Just then, several people entered the restaurant. They were all dressed in black, and you could tell they were unfortunate also and had been crying.

A beautiful older lady walked up to the table, looked at Joe, and said, "Come on, hubby, we have to get to the train station. We just got a call, and Diane's coffin just came in and is at the station."

The old man got up, looked directly at John and Kate, and said, "You two have a good time in West Virginia, and don't wait ten years before coming back." He then put his arm around his wife and walked out of the restaurant with the rest of the people.

John looked at Kate, and there were tears in both their eyes, and he said, "I am so happy that we were able to spend as much time as we have with our daughter. We are so lucky that she now has this cancer under control."

Kate responded, "That man was so nice to share that gift about his daughter with us. It makes you appreciate what you have. The people here are so nice." John and Kate just stayed at the table holding hands, sipping their coffee, having some breakfast, and looking at the beautiful Cheat River.

After breakfast, Kate said, "So when you run today, how far will you go, and what are you listening to these days on your cassette."

"You know, I always do about six miles when running. I listen to a tape cassette and practice the country's language that I will be visiting when I start my run and then when I turn and I am on my way back from my run I listen to music or sports on the radio. This week it is Spanish. I am finding that this is a good way to learn different languages.

This past year I have been stopping in the middle of the run. It is usually at a place where there is a clear view of the sky and if it is by a river or mountains that is even better. It is a place where I know God is listening. At that time, I thought about everything that was good that I knew he would not want me to change. I also think about things that I need help with and pray for that help to come. The help does not come all the time, but I figure that is because he does not believe that is what I should have anyway. So far, we have been lucky because what has come for us is health and happiness."

Kate said, "You know, I think our love grows stronger the longer we are together."

"I feel the same way, Kate."

"Well, I better head off on my run, or we will not get to do any shopping. I need to go up to the room, put on some sun tan oil, get my hat and get my cassette recorder."

Kate said, "I think I will stay here for a while and have another cup of coffee and watch the Cheat River. It seems like an ideal place to relax."

John tried to get ready for his run quickly so he could catch a view of Kate before he started his run. He did what he needed to do in the room and then was out the hotel lobby door in just a few minutes. Once he was outside, he then tried to find the restaurant's window where Kate was sitting.

When he saw Kate in the restaurant, he tried to get her attention. When he did, he smiled and waved. She smiled, stood up, and waved back. John was always trying to make Kate smile. It made him feel good when she felt good.

He then went over to the running path and started his run. It was a beautiful run. The river was on one side and the woods and mountains on the other.

He was close to the end of the run, and in the distance, he saw two helicopters coming down the Cheat River toward the lodge. It was a beautiful sight. Air Force helicopters coming down the river with mountains on both sides. As the helicopters neared the lodge, John began to run faster in order to get to the lodge before the helicopters landed.

The helicopters made such a loud noise that Kate and several other people staying at the lodge were on the porch trying to see what was happening.

The helicopters landed on a small heliport that was on the side of the lodge in an open area. John arrived at the lodge before the people got out of the helicopters. John saw Kate on the porch and walked up to her. They both smiled at each other and held hands. They were always holding hands. Then John said, "I wonder what this is all about?"

Then John recognized one of the people as his old boss, Jim McCallum. Jim was tall and a distinguished-looking African American man. He looked similar to James Earl Jones. He was married and had two children. Jim is the White House Chief of Staff. For the last five years, he's had that position and has worked directly with three different United States Presidents in various jobs. He is well respected all over the world.

Jim always used John and Kate on the country's most important projects. They have worked in different branches of the government, but Jim always had the power to get them when he needed them. He trusted them and knew they would give their all on every project. Also, all of their projects usually turned out well. Jim often said that they both could focus on items better than anyone he had ever known and reach any goal set upon them.

He was a boss and a friend to both Kate and John. The last project that they worked on for Jim was the Medical Project. Jim had this project under him because his agency went across many agencies, it was one of the President's special projects, and it was a worldwide project.

He was a person that understood Washington Politics. People that worked for Jim liked him. He has spoken to congress and the senate many times and not only has the respect of those bodies but also the President.

Jim, two security guards, and his executive assistant got out of the helicopters. They had their heads down because the blades from the helicopter were still turning slowly. The four Air force pilots flying the helicopters all stayed in the helicopters.

At a distance, Jim smiled and waved at John and Kate. The four came up to the porch where John and Kate were standing. Jim came right up to them and hugged John and then Kate and then said, "How is your daughter Katelin doing?"

Kate responded, "She is doing better."

Jim then said, "You both are looking good. How are you both doing?"

John responded, "We are doing OK. It is good to see you again. Why all the hoopla, and who are these people with you?"

"You know I always had an Executive Assistant that tags along with me. This Executive Assistances name is Doris Smith. The other two people are security guards."

Jim usually has one of his brightest young people be an Executive Assistant for about a year so that the person will get an understanding of the entire organization. This gets them ready for the next important position in the organization.

"I understand the Executive Assistant, but why the security guards and the two helicopters."

There were still people on the porch looking at Jim. Some did not know who he was, but some wondered why the Chief of Staff to the President would be in West Virginia at this lodge.

Jim got a serious look on his face, got a little closer to John and Kate, and asked, "Can we spend some time together. There is something I need to discuss with you. After we talk, you will understand the reason for the hoopla. Do you think we can find a more private place where we can talk?"

Kate quickly looked around and then suggested, "Let's sit at that table over by the trees. It is in a secluded spot and in the shade."

As they were walking to the table, Kate asked Doris to tell a little about herself. The security guards remained close so they would have a complete view of the entire area. The pilots stayed in the helicopters.

Doris looked at Kate, smiled, and said, "OK, I have heard a lot about you and John, so let me tell you about myself. I am thirty years old and started working for the government after I received my legal degree. I am single and started out in the research department and have had a few successful projects within the government."

Kate responded, "It sounds like you are doing OK. Do you like your work?"

"I love the work and like working for Jim and his team."

They all got to the table, and then Jim looked directly at John and Kate, saying, "Why don't you both sit directly across from Doris and me." The table would allow four people to sit at it. Once they were all seated, Jim looked directly at both John and Kate and said, "The agency needs your help, and the President of the United States asked me to find you and explain the situation personally. The President knows that you are the best to lead this project, and he is asking for your help. He wants you to help get the Medical Project restarted."

John looked at Jim and was upset when he responded, "Listen, Jim, you know we left the agency because the worldwide Medical Project was killed, and there was no sound reason for killing the project. We do not want to get involved again in working on something that could be killed after putting our hearts and souls into it.

The upsetting thing is that you know this system would have allowed people and doctors to benefit worldwide. The end result would allow people and doctors to see what needs to be done to cure any disease. This system would help individuals deal with a particular type of cancer and would recommend all the treatments for the specific cancer they have. It would also give results of those treatments and where people should go to get the best treatment, and it would be available to anyone.

It would allow cures for all diseases to be more effective around the world. In addition, if a new disease would pop up anywhere in the world, people would know about it and be able to work on a cure and isolate the disease before it spreads. An example of this would be acquired immunodeficiency syndrome (AIDS) and coronavirus disease of 2019(COVID-19). If AIDS and COVID-19 could have been detected when they first started, they could have been isolated and a cure would have been put together before they spread.

Doris looked at Kate, a little surprised, and said, "Why would we cancel a project like this? When was the project scheduled to end? Additionally with find cures for many diseases and also finding the best cures for diseases, it would reduce the cost of all medical care. This will help people on medicare and all other people. Medicare will not run out of money as predicted but will give money back."

Kate responded quickly, "The project was put together so that within five years, we would be able to uncover new diseases and wipe out diseases that we have today. It was announced similar to how we announced the space program and put people on the moon. After about three years, the President and Congress killed this project because of lobbyists in the medical industry."

John looked at Jim again and asked, "Are there any countries that continued with the project?"

"There were a few countries that continued the project but at a slower pace. Even though they continued, the system would not be as effective due to the much smaller historical database. You know that if you have fewer doctors inputting ways they cured cervical cancer or any other disease then there is less of a chance of finding a cure. There is a better chance that you will find the cure with more doctors inputting information. It is a shame since some parts of the system were close to being complete. We would have been further along with cures if we did not stop the work."

Doris asked, "What were some details on how the system would work and how many lives would it have saved? It seems like something I would like to work on with you after I finish my current assignment."

John went on to explain," It was estimated that the number of lives saved per year would be in the millions, and the quality of life would improve. The project had five stages, and over time the number of lives saved would be increased after each stage was complete and also as the database grew.

The first stage would have the doctors or assistants input information into the computer systems. All diagnoses will be made by the doctor and assisted by the computer. This would mean that doctors all over the world would input information into a central database.

Based on the information entered, a diagnosis would be recommended by the computer. If the doctor agreed, then the doctor would use that diagnosis. This would be like a second opinion from a doctor. If the doctor did not agree, they would go with their diagnosis and input it into the computer. This would allow the computer to get smarter.

The computers would also recommend a fee that should be paid to each person involved in the patient's care.

The second stage would allow the patient to input information into the system. This would be based on lab tests received or the family's history.

The patient could then make a diagnosis with the doctor's assistance. The patient could enter into the system things they think they have wrong and what pain they have and the doctor can then ask the patient to come to the office for further analysis or give a diagnosis and send the pharmacist a prescription.

Doctors must use the system, but if the ill person does not want to go to the second or future stages, they can stay with stage one.

The third stage would allow for devices to be made that would scan the body and input information into a computer, and then diagnosis to be made with a doctor's supervision. You have seen some of these devices in the store today. Allowing patients to take their temperature, blood pressure, and test blood.

Well, the future devices will allow us to do x-rays, test blood, and many other things which would allow you to detect cancer and other diseases. This would allow us to uncover diseases at an early stage since it would be inexpensive to use, and everyone would have one.

The fourth stage would allow for prescriptions or cures to be made automatically based on diagnosis from computer and doctors' approval. If the doctor wanted to override the computer, they would have to justify why it was wrong. The larger machines or devices in the hospital that must be used for curing diseases will have more availability since diseases will be cured in the early stages.

It is estimated that this will allow patients to communicate more with doctors and stop the escalating cost of medical treatment. In all cases, money does not enter into methods of diagnosis. Only the best method of curing the illness is the consideration, which is determined by the history of past cures.

The fifth stage would have the system make a diagnosis based on patient input and direct the patient to the best service provider in their area and also outside their area. The doctors will monitor the system occasionally to make sure the system is operating correctly. This means that the best specialist and hospitals will be getting most of the business.

Doris, this is an overview of the system. Does this give you an idea of how it would work?"

"Yes, thank you, John. Jim, if it is OK with you, I am now sure this is something I want to be involved with after my assignment with you."

Jim appreciated the conversation that was going on, but wanted to try to get everyone back on track and get an answer to his question concerning help from John and Kate, so he said, "Doris, I think we will all be involved with this project. Kate, the agency needs you and John to help with this global problem. The people that are working on the system now are being killed. The people that were in Paris, Tokyo, and Singapore were killed.

All of those countries were still working on the project. I believe that someone or some group does not want the Medical Project to see the light of day and they are killing people still working on the project. The world was hoping that one country would finish and test the system and then sell it to the other countries or the United States would take the lead on the project. At this point, if everyone working on it is being killed then the Medical Project will be stopped worldwide. Each President in the countries that had their Medical Project leaders killed has called the President and asked him to help."

Kate looked at Jim and said with a firm look on her face, "John and I have discussed this many times, as John said, and we do not want to get involved. John told you we took a leave from our government jobs because the project was killed. Jim, you also know that we have stopped working on the project to spend more time with our daughter, Katelin, who is battling cancer."

"I thought you said that Katelin was doing better."

A tear came to Kate's eye, and she said, "She is doing better now and that is why we are here. She is now going through some tests this weekend at the hospital. Before this weekend, we were both with her every day. We were taking her to the doctor's offices for treatment daily. She was getting chemo-therapy. This therapy had just concluded. They were checking her in the hospital to verify if they got all the cancer.

She has been battling this cancer problem for over a year. This past year we have only focused on Katelin getting better. The three of us are closer than we have ever been because we have been focused on solving this problem."

For a brief moment, there was a stop in the conversation. Then John told a brief story about Katelin, "Before Katelin got cancer, she was one of the youngest executives in her company. She modeled when she was in High School and breezed through college. Everyone would tell us she looked just like her mother.

When she graduated, she got a job immediately and had fifty people working for her within a year. She was a person that could do anything and was liked by everyone.

Within her company, she was on the fast track to becoming an executive. She continued to move up the ladder within her company, and then she got this cancer. Now she is on leave from her company and working hard to rid herself of this cancer.

We know that our daughter would have been diagnosed earlier if the Medical Project had been started earlier and allowed to be completed. It would have been caught at an early stage by just inputting information into the computer. The computer would then have enough information to indicate Katelin as a risk for her type of cancer. This would be based on her family history, her current lifestyle, and the new test done by her doctor and her.

Some of these new tests were usually done by doctors but could be done by patients. These new devices that patients could use were being designed before the project was killed. She then could use some of the new devices that are being designed to detect cancer and work with the doctors to confirm the diagnosis. The system would then recommend how to treat cancer and where to go for the treatment.

Kate then said, "We are not happy with the way the government is handling the medical industry in this country and around the world. We are upset with the President, the Congress, the Senate and also you Jim for killing the project.

The US was putting in most of the money for the project and when US backed out, most other countries stopped development. This system, if built, could have helped our daughter and many other people throughout the world, but it was stopped because some organizations and people who are making money off the way the medical industry is being run today would lose money. So, Jim, I hope you understand why we do not want to get involved in the Medical Project. "

Jim responded, "The President thought you would say no and asked if both of you would talk to him directly before making a final decision. He would like to see both of you tonight if possible, and the President would appreciate it if you would stay at the White House. The President knows you are the best people for this project, and he wants you both to lead the restart of the project."

John looked at Jim with a smile and said, "When you put it that way, Jim, it is hard to say no."

John and Kate looked directly into each other's eyes. Kate then nodded, affirming she had no problem. Their two hearts always seemed to beat as one. They are usually on the same page on everything that matters.

John then responded to Jim, "OK, we will go to see the President. Wait a few minutes. We need to pack a few items before we leave."

Jim looked at both John and Kate with a big smile and said, "OK the President is going to be very happy. We mustn't delay since there have been deaths of people working on the project today, and the President is concerned about others currently working on the project. He will give you more details later."

They all got up from the table and walked to the front door of the hotel and then into the lobby. The security guards followed them. As they were walking toward the hotel, Jim told one of the guards to tell the pilots that we would be going back to Washington in about thirty minutes. One of the security guards went inside the hotel, and the other went to the pilots and told them to get things ready and then walked to the front door and stood guard just outside the front door. At that time, Jim called the White House and let the President know that John and Kate were coming. He also briefed him on their concerns.

John and Kate went up the stairs to their room. Jim and Doris waited for them in the lobby area. The lobby had a big fireplace and several couches which faced the fire place. Jim sat on one of the couches, and the bodyguard that was inside was standing off to the side near the door.

Upstairs while John and Kate were trying to decide what to bring. John stopped packing, turned and looked at Kate, and asked, "Did Jim ever have two bodyguards with him when he was traveling in the United States?"

Kate responded with a worried look on her face and responded, "No, he never had a bodyguard, but he did mention that there were killings in other countries. I am concerned that this is more than just a restart of the Medical Project. The bodyguards and the door-to-door helicopters would indicate this will be more difficult than just completing the Medical Project."

After about 30 minutes, John and Kate had completed the packing of a couple of overnight bags. They came down the stairs to the lobby and went to the desk. John recognized the person behind the desk as the person that checked them in and said, "We will not be staying the night but will be back tomorrow."

The desk manager responded, "That gentleman over there took care of everything." He was pointing at Jim.

Just then Jim walked quickly up to the desk, looked directly at John and said, "Listen John, the government is interrupting your vacation. We will pick up the total bill. While you were upstairs, I took care of things with the hotel manager."

John responded, "Thanks Jim."

They all walked out the lobby door, and Jim pointed to the helicopter closest to the lodge and said, "Why don't you and Kate go in that helicopter, and Doris and I will go in the other one." A security guard went in each of the helicopters. As soon as Kate, John, and one of the security guards were in the helicopter, the door was closed, and the engines started. Within thirty seconds, both helicopters were lifting off.

John mentioned to Kate, "We have made the flight from West Virginia to Washington D.C. many times but never in a helicopter."

Kate responded, "This is exciting. I have never seen Jim look so worried. Doris seems like a nice person. I think I will ask her out for coffee when we get back to Washington."

John and Kate just held hands during the trip and looked out the window. As they passed points of interest, they pointed them out to each other. The helicopter landed right next to the White House, and the President was waiting outside on the lawn to greet them.

John and Kate thought that Jim must have briefed the President since he was waiting for them. John, Kate, Jim, and Doris got out of the helicopters and went up to the President. When John and Kate got in front of the President, he looked directly at them, smiled, and said, "It is nice to see you both again. I am so happy that you were able to break away from your vacation."

John smiled at the President and said, "This is the first time we ever stayed at the White House. Kate and I appreciate the invitation. Jim explained the situation to us when we were in West Virginia. It is tough to believe that this could be happening."

The President looked at both of them and was very serious when he said, "This is an unusual time we live in, and there are some people that will do anything for money, but let's wait until dinner, and we can discuss this in more detail. Jim, can you and Doris join us?"

"Yes, I would be happy to join in. How about you, Doris?"

"Yes, I can make it also. What time?"

The President smiled and responded, "Let's plan on having dinner at 7:30 p.m. That will give everyone a chance to rest. By the way, the first lady is not here today. She had to visit her mother, who is ill. It will just be the five of us."

Jim and Doris proceeded to the West Wing of the White House, where their offices were located. The two security guards that were in the helicopter followed them.

John and Kate followed the President and security guards into the White House. Two people were waiting for the President once they were inside the door. One looked like the butler, and the other came up to the President and said, "Mr. President, I need to talk with you for a moment."

The President responded, "OK, just a moment. Kate and John, can you follow the butler and he will show you where you will be staying tonight. I will see you at dinner tonight."

Kate and John were taken to the Lincoln bedroom. When they got to the bedroom with a smile, John looked at Kate and said, "Can you believe where we are?"

Kate also had a smile on her face and said, "I cannot believe it. What do you think we should say to the President when he asks us if we want to restart the Medical Project?"

"First, I think we should call Katelin and let her know where we are and see how the tests are going. If she is doing better then maybe we should consider helping the President. Why don't you give her a call Kate?"

"I was thinking the same thing."

Kate then picked up the phone. When she did, she got the main switchboard to the White House, gave them the hospital's number, and asked them for Katelin's room. When Katelin got on the phone Kate said, "Katelin, you will not believe where your father and I are now."

"The lodge in West Virginia?"

"Wrong! We are in the White House, in the Lincoln bedroom."

"You must have given a big donation to the President! Make sure you take some towels. I can't believe it. I talked to you yesterday, and you were in West Virginia. What did you two do wrong that made the government take you away from your vacation and bring you to the White House?"

"It seems the President and Jim want us to help them with a project. What do you think about that?"

"Do it!"

"How are the tests going?"

"No cancer, but I still have a little pain. I am fine."

"Mom, I think you should take the job. I plan to go back to work this coming week. Let me speak to dad."

"OK, just a minute. Katelin wants to speak to you." Kate handed John the phone.

John took the phone and said, "Hey sweetie, how are you doing?"

"I am doing fine, daddy. I want you and mom to take this job. I will be fine. I am feeling a lot better."

"OK, we are going to get more information about the job. If taking the job is the right thing to do, then we will do the job. Thanks, honey. I am really happy about the test. Here is your mom."

"Hey, mom, what do you think I should wear to my first day back to work?"

"I like the black and white suit on you."

"OK, it is the black and white suit. So how does it look inside the White House?"

"Your dad and I cannot believe we are here. We keep looking at ourselves in disbelief. We are having dinner with the President and we are going to sleep in the White House. A couple of ordinary people in the White House."

"Yeah, mom! When are you and dad going to realize how good you both are and how important the work is to the country?"

"Thanks, Katelin. I would expect that from our daughter. We love you."

"OK, mom, I look forward to seeing you guys on Monday. Take

good notes. I will have a lot of questions about the White House."

Kate hung up the phone, looked at John with tears in her eyes, and said, "You know we are fortunate to have such a great daughter. I think we should take the job. What do you think?"

"I am with you, and I think we have done all we can for Katelin. She seems to be OK. We need to get out and start working with our friends again and finish what we started. It will make us feel better about ourselves.

Actually, if we can complete the Medical Project, we will be helping a lot of people. Let's see what Jim and the President have to say, and if they guarantee to restart the Medical Project and not stop it until we complete it, then we should help make that happen.

I think this leave has done us good. We have had a chance to understand how fragile life is and how important it is to complete this project."

Kate responded, "I agree. We can now look at what good this will bring the world. It will make a difference in the way people live today."

Kate went into the bathroom to freshen up while John sat on the bed, and then Kate came out and said, "When we are discussing this tonight, let's try to understand if there is a safety problem. We just got Katelin healthy, and I don't want anything to happen to you."

"The sooner we find the person doing the killing the sooner we will be safe. I think we are lucky they have not come after us. Whoever is doing the killing must have realized that we would be asked to join the project and be coming after us. We were just lower on the list of people they were planning on killing."

They rested for a while, and then, around 7 p.m. Kate turned to John, smiled, and said, "We better get ready. We don't want to keep the President waiting."

They both changed what they had on and got ready. John then said, "OK, are you ready?"

Kate looked at John and said, "Let's go."

John opened the door to the room, and the butler was standing there and said, "May I escort you down to the dining room?"

John responded, "You read my mind. We are ready."

The man walked in front of John and Kate. They followed, holding hands. They all proceeded to the dining room. When they arrived, they noticed the President was standing in one corner of the dining room drinking a glass of wine with Jim and Doris.

When the President saw John and Kate enter the dining room, he went directly to them. Jim and Doris followed. The President asked John and Kate, "What would you like to drink?"

Kate looked at what everyone else was drinking and said, "I will have what you are drinking."

John responded, "Me too."

The President then waved at the person that was pouring and said, "Two more glasses of wine."

He brought over two more glasses of wine. Kate and John both took a sip of wine and John said, "This is an excellent wine. What kind of wine is it?"

The President responded, "It is Beringer, White Zinfandel. My wife and I like it and usually have it when we have friends visit the White House."

All five of them were standing in the dining room talking when the table was being made ready for dinner. Every now and then a person would come over and pour some wine and bring over some appetizers.

The President smiled and told John and Kate, "I am delighted that you and Kate could come to the White House. It was a mistake to kill the project. When it was time to go for stage 2, we needed to get the funding authorization from Congress and the Senate. As much as we tried to get the funding, they said they would not authorize the funding."

Jim quickly added to what the President was saying, "I suspect lobbyists were working on people within the Congress and the Senate to vote against the funding. Since we knew it would get discontinued, we decided to shift focus to another project and let the other countries devise a solution.

We thought that when the other countries got close to completing the project, we could get back into the picture. But now, if people working on the project continue to be killed, we will never see the project completed."

The President said, "During the campaign, I told everyone I would revamp the medical field. The Medical Project was something I needed to get done to keep my promise. When I discontinued the project, I let down the people that voted for me. Now it is affecting countries all over the world that decided to continue working on the project. I have received calls from all the countries that are still working on the project. They want our help. People in the Congress, Senate, and the United Nations are also getting calls from their friends all over the world concerning the Medical Project."

As soon as the President paused, Jim spoke up quickly, saying, "This has now become a world problem that we need to fix. We have struck a deal with Congress and the Senate, and they have agreed to fund the US portion of the whole project and there will be no stopping this time until it is completed. You know the President and I have always wanted the project to continue, and now we have everyone on our side."

The President then switched subjects and asked, "How is Katelin doing in her battle with cancer?"

Kate said, "We just talked with her on the phone. Every time they think they have things under control, some other cancer shows up in some place in her body. Right now, the doctors are saying the cancer is in remission, and she is checking out of the hospital. So things are looking good right now, and she is in a lot better shape than she was a year ago. She cannot believe we are here and wants us to bring her something with the White House seal."

The President said, "That is great! I want to give you three White House packages. One for each of you to keep and the other for Katelin. It is just a couple of towels, a bathrobe, and some toilet articles with the White House emblem. I know that you and John left the agency to go on leave because the project was canceled and because of Katelin's cancer. If things are looking better concerning the cancer, and we have an agreement to restart the Medical Project, would you and John consider coming back from leave and working with us on this problem and restarting the project?"

Kate said, "When we talked with Katelin, she told us to come back on the project. John and I believe it is the right thing to do also. What do you think, John?"

"I would say yes under certain conditions. We may need to take some time off to be with Katelin if she has a problem. Also, we will need bodyguards. This person that is killing people has a lot of money and influence. Also, people working in other countries on this project will need body guards immediately. If we agree on those items, then we will come back on the project."

The President and Jim looked at each other, and Jim nodded his head, indicating he was OK, so the President said, "The conditions are very reasonable, I agree. Let's get started. I am giving you and Kate full responsibility for the project and also would allow both of you to get whatever is needed to get the job done. Jim, you need to keep me updated weekly.

Now that we got that out of the way let's all sit down and have some dinner. Kate, I believe you are a vegetarian, and they prepared a special meal for you. The rest of us can have some surf and turf."

They all walked over to the table. The President sat at the head of the table. Doris and Kate were on either side of the President, John sat next to Kate, and Jim sat across from John. Everyone then began eating.

The President stopped eating for a moment and then looked at John and Kate and said, "John, Kate, we picked both of you because you have done a good job for us on a past project and you know all the players on this project.

You also know the people that helped promote the project and also the people that would be against the project. Maybe you can help us find the person responsible for all the killings.

We need the best people on this project so we can get it done quickly. It is the most important project that we have in our nation today. Thank you for helping us get this done."

John responded, "Mr. President, we will get the person responsible for the deaths. This is a program that needs to be successful."

Doris asked John, "What are your plans for starting the project?"

"Kate and I will need to put that together quickly. We should have an initial cut of the plan by Tuesday next week."

The conversation continued for about an hour until everyone completed eating their dinner. Starting a project is always the best time, and everyone had a great dinner. All had a good time. When dinner was done, they all got up, and the president looked and John and Kate and said, "Sorry, I will not be able to join you for breakfast tomorrow morning. I will be going out of town to be with my wife at her mother's house. When would you both like to have breakfast? We will also make arrangements to have the helicopters take you back to the lodge in West Virginia.

John answered, "Let's plan on going back to the lodge at ten tomorrow morning and have breakfast at about eight-thirty. Kate and I can work at the lodge until Monday. We can fly back on Monday and be at the agency on Tuesday."

Jim, with a look of concern, made a comment. "Mr. President, John is correct in saying that he and Kate will need a bodyguard. I am not sure where they were on the list of people who were going to be killed, but I am sure they were on the list.

As soon as word gets out that John and Kate are on the project, then the person responsible for all the killings will move them to the top of their list of people to kill. I believe we will need to put some bodyguards on them immediately.

The President responded, "I agree."

Jim then turned to John and Kate and said, "If it is OK with you, I will have security follow you back to West Virginia. Also, I will have a helicopter transport you to West Virginia and back to Washington DC."

John responded, "That is OK with us."

The President then said, "Does anyone want coffee or dessert?"

John usually runs six miles a day so he can have dessert, so he asks the President, "What kind of dessert are we talking about?"

The President responded, "What would you like? You know this is the White House, and we have a pretty good kitchen."

John said, "How about hot apple pie and vanilla ice cream? I will also have decaf coffee."

The President looked at a person standing beside him and the person shook his head as being affirmative, saying "We have it."

John responded, "Great!"

The President looked around the table, and everyone shook their head in the affirmative, indicating they wanted the same thing, so the President said, "OK, everyone will have hot apple pie and vanilla ice cream. You know this means we will all have to exercise a little extra tomorrow."

After dessert and coffee, the President said, "Thank you all for sharing dinner with me. Great food and great friends, this was a great evening. Welcome aboard, John and Kate." The President then pointed to the butler and said, "John, this gentleman will show you and Kate up to your room. Jim, I will walk you and Doris to the door."

Everyone got up from the table and said good night. The butler then took John and Kate to their room, and the President showed Doris and Jim to the door.

GETTING STARTED

The next morning John and Kate had breakfast in their bedroom in the White House. It was almost like staying at a hotel with room service. After breakfast, they got dressed and packed everything. They opened the door, and a butler was standing at their door with three packages.

The Butler said, "The President thought your daughter and each of you could use one of these guests' packages."

John and Kate laughed, thanked him for the package, and told him they were ready to go. He then guided them through the White House to a door which would exit them to where the helicopter was waiting. When they opened the door and stepped outside, two bodyguards were waiting for them. One of the bodyguards took their luggage, and they all walked to the helicopter.

John and Kate recognized one of the security guards from past jobs. His name was Bill Collins. Bill was a West Point graduate, a green beret, and was married with two children.

He worked with Kate and John when they were in Brazil about two years ago and he spoke Portuguese and several other languages. Kate and John also had him to their house a couple of times for dinner.

When they saw Bill, John said, "Bill, it is so nice to see you again. Kate and I already feel a lot safer."

Bill put a big smile on his face and then responded, "Thanks, John, it is a joy working with you and Kate."

As they approached the helicopter, one of the pilots stepped outside the helicopter. The pilot and the bodyguards then took all the luggage and stored it in the back of the helicopter. After the luggage was loaded, they then all got in the helicopter.

In the helicopter, John, said to Kate "I think I will go for a run when we land. Do you want to come along?

"No, but make sure you take Bill with you. I think I will give Katelin a call and give her an update and find out how she is doing. After that maybe we can discuss the project in the open lodge area that looks like a Hemingway room and then go for dinner."

John had a questioning look on his face and said, "That's a plan. Why are you calling that room the Hemingway room?"

Kate smiled at John and said, "Do you remember the furniture we saw at the Hemingway house in Key West, Florida? Well, they look the same."

Agreeing with Kate, John replied, "That will be a good spot to work. It also has a great view of the Cheat River and the forest."

During the flight everyone enjoyed the view of the mountains and dense forest of West Virginia. When the helicopter landed at the lodge, a few people came out to see who was in the helicopter, but when they did not recognize anyone, they went back into the lodge.

After the helicopter blades stopped, everyone got out of the helicopter, got their suit cases, locked up the helicopter, and walked to the registration desk.

The manager came to the desk and told John, "We got a call from Washington, and everything has been taken care of. We reserved a room on either side of yours, Mr. Colombo. One is for your pilots, and the other is for your bodyguards. Here are the keys to the rooms."

John gave everyone their keys and then smiled at the manager and said, "Thank you for everything, and I am sorry about all the excitement we have created."

Bill then asked everyone to come over to an area of the lobby before they all went to their rooms and said, "One of the bodyguards will be outside the room all day and night. We will change every five hours, and when we do, we will check the grounds outside. We have four walkie-talkies, one for each of you and us. We also want you to take this gun. Do you both know how to use a gun?"

John responded, "Yes, we both know how to use a gun. I have a question. I was planning on going for a run today and tomorrow morning. Will that be a problem?"

Bill responded, "No problem, I will tag along with you, and the other guard will remain outside your door to guard Kate." What time do you want to run?"

"Let's meet in the lobby, and we can run at 1 p.m."

The pilot, John, Kate, and the two bodyguards proceeded to the rooms. When they got to the room, Bill said, "Wait a moment, we need to search the rooms for bombs and listening devices before you go into the room."

After checking out the room, John and Kate went in the room, and the security guard stayed outside the door.

As John was changing into his running outfit, he said, "Kate are you going to update Katelin?"

"I was just going to pick up the phone and call her."

"Let me speak to her for a moment before I go running."

"Katelin, is that you? This is Mom. How are you doing?"

"I am fine, Mom. They cannot find any more cancer. How was the White House? Did you take the job?"

"The White House was great, and we took the job. Your dad wants to talk with you before he goes out for a run. So here is your dad."

"Hi, Katelin."

"Hi, Daddy."

"So, you took the job. I think that is great. I know you cannot tell me anything about the job, but did you get me something from the White House, and what did you have for dinner?"

"I had steak and salmon, of course, and your mom had vegetables. The President asked about you, and when we told him we wanted to bring you something from the White House he laughed, and put together a package for you and us. It actually broke the ice before we got into a serious conversation. We miss you and look forward to seeing you on Monday."

"OK, Daddy, have a good run. I am proud of both of you."

"Love you, Katelin. Here is Mom."

John turned to Kate and handed the phone to her, giving her a big smile. She could tell that he loved them both.

"Hi, Mom, are you excited about the job?"

"Yes, we are so excited that we are going to do some work today as soon as Dad gets back from his run. It seems like we always act like kids on projects. We have fun, and we both like a challenge. I can tell you that we will be working on the Medical Project. We are going to restart the project.

It may be dangerous as we restart the project since there are people that do not want it restarted. I am thinking of asking for extra security so we can have someone watching you. Your dad and I will have a security guard on each of us for a while. Do you think you will need one?"

"You guys have worked on some mighty serious projects, and we never needed a security guard. They know I have nothing to add to the project, so they will not go after me. I don't think I will need a security guard."

"OK, we won't request one for you right now."

"Mom, can you pick me up at the hospital at two in the afternoon on Monday? I am ready to leave this place."

"No problem, we have a helicopter that will take us back to Washington and then we will go straight to the hospital."

Katelin was surprised when she said, "A helicopter is taking you to Washington? Is this project that important that you need security guards and a helicopter to take you places? I will be waiting in the lobby. I can't wait until I get back to my apartment."

"Yes, a helicopter. This project will be dangerous for a while and security will be needed for a while. Katelin, we want you to stay with us for a while when you get out of the hospital."

"Mom, I am going back to work on Tuesday, and I have all my things at my apartment. I will stay with you Sunday night, but on Monday, I want to go to my apartment."

"OK, you win. We will see you Sunday. We want to see you as much as we can."

"Bye, Mom, I love you. See you Sunday at two."

Kate had some time before John would get back from his run so she got a pad and pen and started writing down some of her thoughts. She turned on the TV, sat up in bed, and began writing.

Bill and John were running along the path and about three miles into a six-mile run. John asked Bill, "How is your family doing? Do they miss you when you are gone like this?"

"They are doing great. Short trips like this are not too bad. When I have to be gone for a month or more, it makes it hard on the family. I have been lucky. I have been on projects in the Washington area. So, I can still help around the house and with the kids."

John asked Bill, "How do you keep yourself in shape?"

"Many people I am assigned to guard exercise a lot like you, so when I am on the job, I do get some exercise. I also try to get to the gym and keep my carb intake down. I find if you keep fit, you feel better, and it keeps you sharper."

John smiled at Bill and said, "I don't know about sharper but I do like to eat so I exercise so I can eat what I like. Do you know what you will be assigned to work on after this West Virginia trip? Kate and I would like you to be assigned to our project. Do you think you would like to work on this project?"

"I was going to ask my boss to assign me to this project. We all believe that you and Kate are working on something important for the world. We do not want anything to get in your way."

"Thanks for the support. Kate and I will try to make sure you stay on the project. It may be a little rough initially, but when this project is completed, it will help people all over the world."

"John, you are lucky to be able to work with your wife on some of these projects."

"We are lucky. We don't get to work together all the time, but when projects are this big, we sometimes get assigned to the same project. We work well together and complement each other well. She is the sharpest person I know and really is at her best when there is pressure."

"This is an important project, John. It is a project that will change the world, and the way people do things and make things better than they are today. I have seen you and Kate work together before. What I noticed is that you really complement each other well. I notice that Kate has a good eye for detail, and you both come up with great ideas. Also, when both of you agree on something, then it is golden."

They were getting to the end of their run and John looked at Bill and said, "Thanks, Bill. I appreciate the compliment. The good thing about running with someone is that the run goes by quickly. Thanks for running with me. I am going up to shower, and then Kate and I will be working in an area of the hotel that Kate calls the Hemingway area."

As they went into the lobby, John pointed to the area he was calling the Hemingway area. John and Bill when to their respective rooms, and they both showered. As John went into his room, Kate was getting dressed, and John said, "Kate, you are more beautiful than the day we met. I love you."

"I love you too, John. Hurry up and shower so we can get some work done today. Did you enjoy your run?"

"I enjoyed the run. Bill is a great guy. He wants to work on the project with us. Let's ensure he is on the project list of people we want. Where do you want to eat tonight?"

"Let's try that little place down the road called The Cavern."

"That sounds good to me."

After John's shower, he wore casual clothes, looked at Kate, and said, "Are you ready to go?"

She replied, "Yes."

John then opened the door for Kate and both security guards were there, and they all went down stairs to the Hemingway area. The area had a beautiful brown wooden table, with a phone and two chairs. The chairs were across from each other. Both security guards followed them to the table. They were all standing around the table, and John said to Bill, "When Kate and I are done here, we were thinking of having dinner at about 6 p.m. at a little place down the road called, The Cavern. We can walk there from the lodge."

Bill responded, "That sounds good. I will check it out and make reservations." Then, the other security guard, pointed at a table by the entrance and said, "We can sit at that table and get a good view of the room and also John and Kate."

Kate and John then sat down at the table, and the other security guard stayed at a table on the other side of the room. John then looked at Kate, touched her hand from across the table, smiled, and started by saying, "This is the most important part of the project. We need to lay out the people we require for this project to succeed. If we put together the right team, then our job will be a lot easier. Also, we should try to keep the project office in Washington and keep the main project office small. Who do you think we should have in the project office?"

"Some people started the project with us when it began about four years ago. I think we should make sure that those people are on the team. I definitely think we need Paul Darma. He was the first person we brought on the team. What do you think?"

John, with great excitement in his eyes, said, "I think yes! I was going to give him a call this week. Let's call him right now and see how he is doing and if he is available to work on the project."

John got Paul's phone number in his wallet, picked up the phone, got an outside line, and called Paul on his private line. Paul is a doctor they first met in their first year of college. John used to study with Paul all the time. Whenever John and Kate used to go out on dates, at least half of the time, it was a double date with Paul and the girl he was dating. Who thought that John who was in Pre-Engineering and Paul was in Pre-Medical and just having fun would turn out to be an Engineer and a Doctor?

They used to talk about everything and when Paul had to decide on a specialty, he consulted with John, and without thinking twice, John told him to go into Psychiatry since Paul liked working with people. After Paul got his Medical Degree, he specialized in Psychiatry and became a psychiatrist.

When the project started, John and Kate asked Paul to join the project. Paul was excellent in brainstorming sessions. He was one of the people that came up with the structure that would allow doctors to input information into the data base. He would talk with doctors around the world, and they all respected Paul's opinions.

Paul is a person that would support John and Kate in every way. In fact, he was the best man at their wedding. Recently he found out that he was human immunodeficiency virus (HIV) positive. This was another reason why Paul wanted to ensure this project was successful. He knew there would be future diseases like acute immune deficiency syndrome (AIDS), and if this system were in place, we could stop it before it spread. Paul became infected when he was working with a patient in the hospital.

When John got him on the phone, John said, "Paul, this is John. How are you feeling?"

Paul responded, "I am feeling great. What are you and Kate doing these days?"

"Well, funny, you should ask. That is why we are calling. The President has asked us to restart the Medical Project, and we want you to be on the team doing the same thing you were doing before. This time we guarantee that there is money to complete the project.

We have some work to do before we restart the project. The first is to put together a list of people we need on the project, and your name is at the very top. That is the reason for this call. We both want you to complete this project with us. When can you start?"

Paul was excited and responded, "I want to be a part of this effort. I want to help you guys all I can, and maybe it will help us find a cure for AIDS before it is too late for me.

I often think that if we had this system when the AIDS disease first started, we would have been able to find out about the disease as soon as it broke out and been able to contain it and stop it from spreading and maybe find a cure. We were coming up with the method of having doctors report information just before the project was stopped. We were just getting agreements from doctors concerning how they would report information.

Once we have the information in our systems, the systems would be able to set the alarm as soon as the same disease was detected more than a specified number of times. Once this alarm went off, a team would be dispatched to try to understand what needed to be done to contain it.

You can tell I am excited about this project. You asked when I could start. I would like to start today, but I can't just leave my practice, so I need to have my partner take care of my practice while I am gone. Also, I will need to continue being the principal doctor for a few patients. I should be able to take care of this and be at work next week. Should I go to the West Wing area when I am ready to start?"

"Yes, go to the West Wing. Kate is sitting next to me, cheering silently. We are both excited, and it will be fun working together again. Did you want to say hello to Kate?"

"Yes, put Kate on the line!"

"OK, here's Kate. Take care, and see you next week."

John handed the phone to Kate and she was excited when she came on the line and said, "Hello Paul, I am so happy you can help us."

Paul responded, "I think this project helps all of us. You know I would work on any project that you and John are leading. It will be an honor to work on the Medical Project. How is Katelin doing, and how are you and John doing?"

"Thank you for asking. First, thank you for speaking to my daughter's doctors and Katelin. You are a great friend. Katelin's cancer is in remission, and we are all doing great."

"That is great news. You let me know if there is anything I can do for Katelin, you, or John. You know cancer is something that affects the whole family. It affects the person who has it and everyone close to that person. I look forward to working with you and John again."

Kate hung up the phone, turned to John, smiling, and said, "He is a great friend. Do we want him to do the same thing before the project is stopped? I had him as the interface to all the doctors around the world?"

"Yes, it is a big job, but I do not believe there is anyone better for that job than Paul. I think you would have Paul and all the doctors around the world reporting to you and also control Project Offices around the world. That is what we were doing before the project was stopped. Are we in an agreement?"

Kate thought for a moment and then responded, "That sounds OK." Have you thought about who would be responsible for developing the product? We still need to find the right person for that job."

John and Kate discussed who would head up development and did a little more work on the list of people they wanted on the project, and then Bill walked in the room and up to their desk and said, "It is 5:30 p.m. Is everyone ready for dinner? I made the reservations for 6 p.m."

Kate responded, "I am ready. We better get going if we have reservations for six in the evening. John and I need to go upstairs to our room to drop this paperwork off, and then we will meet you all in the lobby."

Bill responded, "I will come upstairs with the both of you. We will all meet in the lobby in about ten minutes."

After about ten minutes, everyone met in the lodge's lobby and went out the front door of the lodge. Once out the door, Bill pointed to the walking path, indicating they needed to get on the path. Bill led the way, and the other security guard followed everyone. Kate and John held hands, and they all started to walk along the path which goes along the river.

This path leads directly to the restaurant, which is located on the river. Once they reached the restaurant's front door, Bill said to John, "I made a reservation for you and Kate to sit at a table overlooking the river. The four of us will be sitting at a table by the door where we have a view of the entire restaurant. I also arranged for a car to pick us up after dinner so we do not have to walk along the path at night."

Bill then led everyone into the restaurant and talked to the person who made the reservation. Everyone was then led to their tables. John pulled back Kate's chair, and she sat down, and then John went over to a chair next to Kate and sat down.

Then he said, "I really like this restaurant. Restaurants close to the university are upbeat. Everyone working at them is a student, so you could be served by one of our up-and-coming doctors, lawyers, or engineers."

John and Kate liked going out together. They usually discuss everything that happened to them that day or things that were on their minds. Lately, the discussion has been around their daughter and shifted to the President and the medical project.

There was a brief moment of silence, and then Kate looked directly into John's eyes and said, "I love you."

John continued looking into her eyes and said, "I love you too, Kate. This calls for a glass of wine and a great meal. Of course, for you, it will be a spinach salad, steamed vegetables, and a great dessert."

Kate responded, "That is a feast for a vegetarian. You can order for me. You know what I like. What are you having?"

"For me, a steak would be a feast." The young waiter came over, and John gave him the order for Kate and himself. When the wine came to the table, John made a toast to Kate, saying, "This is to health and happiness."

They both clicked their glasses and kissed. During dinner, there was a sunset. John and Kate watched the sunset while they ate dinner and talked about the project and Katelin most of the time.

After dinner, John said, "How about an ice cream sundae and a coffee?"

Kate shut her eyes, kissed John on the lips, and said, "You know I would love a sundae and a hot chocolate."

John called the waiter and said, "Two sundaes and two hot chocolates."

John looked over to Bill and the others and just smiled. They all smiled back and gave a little wave. Bill motioned to his stomach, indicating that if John ate that sundae, he might have to run an extra mile tomorrow.

After the sundaes and hot chocolates, the waiter came over to John's table, pointed to Bill's table and said, "The gentleman over at that table said he was picking up dinner for both tables."

John waved his hand to Bill in appreciation, turned to the waiter, said, "Thank you, sir, it was a fine dinner."

John then got up and pulled Kate's chair back so she could get up. "Kate said, "Thank you. You really spoil me when we are away from work."

John said, "I love to spoil you." He kissed her on the cheek.

John and Kate then walked over to Bill's table and said, "Thank you for treating us to a great evening. Are you all ready to go?"

Bill responded, "It was my pleasure, but this weekend is on the government. We just checked, and the limo is waiting outside. We are all ready."

They all got into the Range Rover Sentinel and went back to the lodge. Since there was no direct road back to the lodge, it took a while for the car to get there. It gave everyone a chance to see the area. When they got to the lodge, everyone got out of the car and walked into the lobby.

Once everyone was in the lobby, John stopped and said, "I am going to try to wake up at 6:30 a.m. and go for a run. Our thinking is that we can head back to Washington around 11 a.m. Does that sound OK with everyone?"

Bill responded, "Yes, that would be good. I will be running with you tomorrow morning. If you need anything, one of us will be outside your door at all times."

Everyone then went to their rooms. The two of them felt good and were madly in love, so they went to sleep after making love.

LEAVING WEST VIRGINIA AND PICKING UP KATELIN

The next morning John woke up first at 6:00 a.m. and asked Kate, "How about a run?"

Kate said, "Yes! I feel like a run today. You better let the security guards know that we both will be running today and also breakfast plans."

John opened the door to their room and said, "Good morning, Bill! Kate and I are going for a run in about thirty minutes. Then we may get some breakfast, leave at about 11 a.m. has planned and head back to Washington Airport. From there, we will pick up our daughter at the hospital at two in the afternoon."

Bill responded, "That will work."

John and Kate had a coffee machine in their room, so John made some coffee for both of them, and they both sipped the coffee as they got dressed. At about 6:30 a.m., they went out the door, and Bill was waiting for them.

When John saw Bill, he said, "OK, Bill, we are ready. Let's go." They all went outside and onto the path that ran along the river.

Bill said during the run, "The other day, I was having dinner with a cousin of mine, and he told me that he was not making any money as a doctor and is thinking of doing something else."

John responded with a similar story, "Yeah, I had a small lump removed from my lip. I had to call on five doctors before finding one that would remove the lump. He asked if I knew why I had to call on five doctors before I finally found the one who would do the surgery. I said that I did not know, and he said that this operation doesn't pay anything to the doctor. He said that he would do the operation. Work today is like a hobby for him. He is not making any money.

I thanked him, and we set up a time for the operation. I guess the point behind these two stories is that someone is making a lot of money because it is costing us more for insurance, but the doctors are getting less, and we are also getting less medical help for our money. Hopefully, when we complete our project, the people who deserve the money will get it."

The run went by quickly because John, Kate, and Bill all ended up talking about the project and looking at the beautiful view. When they completed the run, they were at the lodge and then walked in the front door.

Before they went into their rooms and while they were standing in the hall outside their rooms, Kate said, "How about we meet outside our door and go to breakfast in about forty-five minutes."

Bill responded, "Sounds good to me."

Kate and John showered, got dressed, and then left their room as planned in forty-five minutes. When they got outside, they noticed that the pilots and other security guards were there with Bill. Bill turned to John and Kate and said, "Is it ok if everyone joins us for breakfast?"

Kate smiled at the team and said, "Yes, it is ok. Let's try to find a table where we can all sit together."

They then all walked down the stairs to the breakfast room. There was one round table with a great view of the river and mountains, so Bill led everyone to that table. There was no one else in the breakfast room at that time.

Everyone at breakfast talked about the view and what was next on their schedule. John and Kate wanted to get a little work in today and also make sure they left at 11 a.m. so they would be on time to pick up Katelin from the hospital, so they were rushing through breakfast.

After breakfast, John said to Kate, "Should we do our work in the Hemingway area?"

Kate responded, "Let's do it. Bill, we will just be working at the same table we were at yesterday. We will need about one hour so we can finish our packing, check out, and leave.

Bill responded, "I can check everyone out. While you and John work, one of the guards will be at the same table we were at yesterday."

One of the pilots said, "We will be checking out the helicopter for the flight back and meet you all outside when you are ready."

John and Kate then walked to the Hemingway area and sat at the same table they were at the other day. Kate then said, "Let's make sure that we work close to Jim in the West Wing of the White House. I think we will need some offices and a conference room. Also, I believe we should get laptops so we can use the same computer wherever we are in the world. What do you think?

"I believe we should work in the West Wing, and I like the idea of laptops. I think we should call Jim and give him all this information and also the task of getting the people we want."

"Why don't you call him now?"

"OK!" John picked up the phone, dialed Jim's private line, and got him on that line. "Good morning, Jim. Kate and I have been working on a list of people we will need. We also want you to get space for us in the West Wing and some laptops. We sent you an email on all this stuff. You can give Doris some of the logistics work in the note. In fact, she is one of the people we are asking that we put on the team."

"She has already asked me if she can be on the team. I also got a call from Bill's manager asking if he can be on the team."

"Yes, we would like them both. By the way, we also talked with Paul Darma, who has also agreed to be a part of the team."

"That's great. I will make sure we get the computers and people you want. When are you planning on coming into the office?"

"We are flying back today and plan to be in the office on Tuesday."

"That sounds good. John. I will make sure a car picks you up at the airport and takes you where you need to go today. Also, there will be a car at your home on Tuesday."

"Sounds great!"

After the call, it was about 10:30 a.m., so John and Kate got up, walked over to Bill, and said, "We better pack and get back to Washington.

Bill responded, "I will walk you to your door and meet you outside the door after you finish packing."

John and Kate went up to the room and then completed their packing and met Bill, the pilots, and the other guard outside the door and said, "Have you checked us all out of the hotel, Bill?"

"We are all checked out and ready to go."

They all walked to the helicopter. Then they handed the suitcases to one of the pilots. The pilot loaded everything in the back, climbed in the helicopter, and told everyone to fasten their seat belts.

The helicopter then took off and headed back to the Washington DC airport. When the helicopter landed, there was a car waiting. The pilot and the driver loaded their luggage into the car.

There were also two other security guards at the airport to meet them. Bill said to John, "These two guards will be with you and Kate. I will see you tomorrow morning."

Kate said, "Thanks Bill and give my regards to your family."

John and Kate then got into the car with one of the guards. The other guard got into the government car and led the way to the hospital to pick up their daughter, Katelin.

They were running about five minutes late but were very close to the hospital, and Kate said, "John, let's drive right up to the entrance to the hospital. I bet that Katelin has checked out and is waiting for us. She wanted to leave this place. Ah, there she is. You could tell Katelin wanted to leave. She is inside the entrance with her suitcases by her side."

John smiled at his wife and said, "You really know your daughter. She looks great."

Kate and John got out of the car, ran into the lobby, and hugged

Katelin. Kate then took Katelin's hand and said, "We missed you. How do you feel, and what are doctors saying?"

"The doctors are saying they are going to make me a poster girl. They really believe they did a good job. They have all said I made great progress. All of my cancer is gone, and they could not find any other cancer in my body."

They then all left the lobby and went into the car. When they were all seated in the car, Katelin turned to her mom and dad and said with a big smile plastered on her face, "Well, this is nice. You are moving up in the world?"

John changed the subject since he and Kate are embarrassed when someone says something like that. They do like to stay low-key. John then said, "You look great. I hear you're staying at our house tonight. Should we have a pizza party?"

"Sounds good to me, daddy. I got some good news from work. When I got the news from the hospital, I called work and told them I was ready to start working again. They told me they held my job open until I was OK, so I will work tomorrow afternoon as planned. They told me they were looking forward to having me back. Daddy, did mom tell you about me moving back into my apartment after tonight?"

"I am OK with that as long as you are feeling good."

They arrived at the house, and the guard in the car said, "Everyone stays in the car until the other guard has a chance to check the house."

With a look of surprise and worry, Katelin asked her mother, "What is going on here?"

Kate responded, "Don't worry, it is just a precaution since there have been some people getting killed in other countries working on this project, but we should be ok."

With a look of relief, Katelin then said, "OK, I feel a little better, but please don't take any chances. You are the only parents I have."

The guard at the door waved at the car indicating everything was OK. The guard in the car then said, "OK, everyone, follow me."

John, Kate, and Katelin got out of the car and followed the guard to the door. One of the guards stayed outside, and the other followed them into the house.

The guard in the house pointed to the den and said, "Is it ok if I stay in this room close to the front door."

Kate responded, "That room would be fine. We are going to order some pizza. Can I order one for you and your friend?"

The guard responded, "That would be great. Just order us a large pepperoni. Here is $20."

Kate responded, "As long as you are protecting us, we pay for the food. Keep your $20."

The guard responded, "Thank you."

John called the pizza shop and got three large pizzas sent to the house. When the pizza arrived, John invited the guards to join them in the family room for dinner, and the guards declined. One of them grabbed a few pieces of pizza and a coke and ate outside; the other ate inside the den.

Kate, John, and Katelin ate in the family room while watching TV. There was a program on TV that had to do with cancer. They were showing all the various vaccines and chemotherapy which could kill cancer but not kill other cells, and then at the end of the TV show, they said it was not available to everyone.

After John heard some of this, he got annoyed and said to Kate, "Do you believe that they have a cure for some of these cancers but are not coming out with the cure? I bet one of the reasons is that it would put so many other people out of business."

Kate responded, "I would guess it could be any of three things. The first would be that the doctors are not keeping up with the latest cures, the second is that these stories on TV are just not accurate, or third is what you are saying is true. The doctors know about the cures. But since they have all this equipment or drugs they have already paid for, they keep using it rather than using some of the latest cures and scraping their equipment."

Looking very discussed with the whole thing, Katelin said, "I thought the Medical Project would solve this problem. Where are you with the solution?"

John responded, "If the project were not stopped, we would have systems that would have determined the best cures that should be used for any type of cancer, and doctors would have to justify why they are not using the cures."

"Daddy, how would the system know what would be the right cure?"

"Every doctor would be required to enter the problem with a patient and then the cure. The system will find the best cure for a particular illness because it has cured the illness over and over again. After being reviewed by experts, it becomes the cure that must be used unless a doctor has a good reason to deviate. This reason would have to be justified and presented to a group of doctors since it is not the best cure.

It is very logical and has nothing to do with money, equipment, or a cure that a doctor is familiar with. Today a doctor uses the cure he is most familiar with and only goes to conferences a couple of times a year to hear of new cures.

The system brings the latest cures to doctors immediately. The doctors we have talked with think it is great."

"Daddy, can the system be wrong concerning the best cure?"

"Yes, since bodies are all different, a cure may not work on a particular patient, but the system will give percentages on all the possible cures. The one with the highest percentage of people cured is the recommended cure. Secondary cures are also recommended if the primary one does not work.

"Mom, you and Daddy better get this system up and running quickly."

Kate responded, "We can't get started on this part of the project until we find the person trying to stop the world from having the system. After we catch this person, we will then get the system up and running."

Katelin responded with an earnest look, "There are a lot of people counting on you. I just came from a hospital that has rooms full of people taking chemotherapy and radiation. We really need the best way to treat different types of cancer."

John responded, "We are going to do our best, honey."

There was a great deal of conversation that went on between Katelin, John, and Kate. They then decided to get to bed early since they were all returning to work for the first time in the year.

First Day Back at Work in Washington

John woke up early and asked Kate, "You feel like a run today?"

"I think I will skip today's run. I will have breakfast ready when you get back. Be careful."

John put on his running clothes, went to the guard inside his house and said, "I am going for a run in about five minutes. Kate will be staying in the house."

The guard responded, "I will stay here with your wife and let the guard outside know that he should follow you in a car. Neither of us are runners."

John responded, "I will run on the street today so we can stay together."

Five minutes later, John went outside the door and said to the guard, "Ready to go?"

"Yes, I am ready. I will follow behind you."

John smiled and then walked out to the street and started running. He usually runs through a wooded area at the end of his block, but this time he stayed on the street during his run. After about an hour of running, John ended up back at his house. He noticed that the car was outside his house when he arrived. There were two more bodyguards waiting outside his house when he arrived. He noticed that Bill was one of them, and so he went right up to him and said, "Bill, is this the changing of the guards?"

"Yes, when do you want to leave for work?"

"We will leave in about an hour. Kate and I would like to invite you, the other security guard, and the driver in for a cup of coffee and breakfast in about thirty minutes."

"OK, but just coffee."

When John went into the house, he went straight to the bedroom where Kate was dressing. He smiled at Kate and said, "Kate, I invited the car driver and two security guards in for coffee. Can we be ready in thirty minutes? We can leave right after the coffee."

"OK, since this is our first day back to work, I made a list of things you should ensure to bring with you."

"Thanks, Kate, you know me. I would have left half the stuff I needed in the house since I have not been to work in a year."

John asked Kate, "What are you wearing today, and what do you think I should wear."

"I am wearing a suit, and you should probably do the same thing."

John and Kate both got dressed and went out to the kitchen. Kate had already started the coffee machine going and had some toast in the toaster. John told Kate, "I will go get Bill, the other guard, and the car driver. Did you check with Katelin?"

"Last night, Katelin told me not to wake her up in the morning, and she would head off to her apartment later this morning. She does not need to be to work until after lunch."

John went off to get everyone while Kate poured the coffee and got the toast ready. John came back into the kitchen area, which led off to the family room, and said, "OK, everyone, grab a cup of coffee and toast."

Everyone had some coffee and just stood around and talked. Bill asked John, "When should we be ready to take you back home?

"We never know when we will be leaving. My guess is that we will not leave before five but is there a way I can reach when we are ready to leave?

"Here is a walkie talkie. Call me anytime."

After coffee, everyone got into the car and went off to the White House. John turned to Kate and kissed her on the cheek, and said, "This brings back great memories. It should be fun."

The car dropped everyone off at the West Wing of the White House. The security guards stayed outside, and John and Kate went straight to Jim's office. Jim and Doris were in Jim's office making calls to get space in the West Wing for the people John and Kate said they would need. It is never easy to find space and good people to work on a project.

Jim and Doris stopped what they were doing and got up and hugged John and Kate. Jim then said, "Welcome back to the West Wing."

John then pointed to Jim's desk and said, "You keep doing what you are doing. Kate and I are going to put together a short list of countries that could be attacked next. We will also put together a short list of possible people that knew about the project and could be leading the effort to stop the project. This will include a list of lobbyists that could be leading this effort from the US. Jim, have you found an office for Kate and me?"

"I have two offices and a conference room. They are right across the hall. Also, concerning the top priority items to focus on, I have some bad news. When you start putting together the list of countries that have had their leaders on the medical project killed, put England and Mexico on the list. Since we talked to you a couple of days ago, there was an attack on the leaders in England and Mexico. Both of them were killed."

"That is really bad. Kate and I brought those people into the program and knew them well. Thanks for the update, Jim. Based on this, we need to act quickly. We will be working in our offices or conference room if you need us."

John and Kate decided to work in the conference room. They both walked over to the conference room and sat down. They started talking about their plans for the day and weeks ahead.

Kate then got up and started writing down some facts on a whiteboard, and as she was writing, she said, "John, let's go through some history and write down the good things on the project we want to keep and the bad things we want to stop.

As you recall, the President started the project by addressing the United Nations and getting permission to start the project with twenty countries. The size of the country and the amount of data they would have to enter into the database would determine on how much money they would pay each month for the software development.

The medical project office was located under the Chief of Staff because the office had more of a worldwide view. Moreover, this project crossed many agencies and ties into all the countries.

The UN was the method we would use to implement the Medical Project worldwide. The Project Office would disburse all money coming in for research, development, and implementation. Before everything was stopped, you were the president of the worldwide group. No one has been named to replace you. Those things should continue. We need to name you as the president again and put all past rules in place.

People knew the US and four other countries were not working on the project. Five countries that were working on the project have stopped due to their leaders being eliminated. This leaves ten countries that still could have a problem. Those countries could have the key people working on the project killed if someone was trying to stop all work on the Medical Project."

John then said, "Let's look at the five countries that had people killed due to continued work on the project and see if there is a pattern. Each of those countries was a major country in that area of the world. France was the headquarters for work done in Europe. England was also one of the leading countries working on the project in Europe. Japan had the largest number of people in Asia working on the project and was also the headquarters for Asia. Singapore was the headquarters for most of the smaller countries in Asia. Mexico was one of the leaders in Latin America."

Kate said, "Of the ten countries left, I believe that Brazil is the next logical choice for a strike. Brazil is the major country in Latin America, and all the other major countries around the world have already been hit. What do you think?"

"I agree that Brazil is the next place to be hit and have the leader killed. The other place that has the potential to have a problem is Hong Kong. It was a key area because it had some of the smartest people still working on the Medical Project, and it was the gateway into China. I think we need to get this information to Jim and suggest he let the proper people in Brazil and Hong Kong know that they need to get protection for their leaders immediately."

After that discussion, John and Kate went over to Jim's office. They went through the analysis with him and recommended that he contact the appropriate people in the government in Brazil and Hong Kong so they can put security guards on the people working on the medical project.

Jim immediately picked up the phone and started making calls to Brazil and Hong Kong to ensure proper security was immediately given to the people working on the project. John and Kate waved to Jim as he was making the calls, indicating to him they were going back to the conference room.

After lunch, Jim came to the conference room and said, "We did some background checks on people running the operation in Hong Kong and Brazil. Over 800 people are working on the project in Brazil.

John, you let a person go when you were on the project. That person had his house broken in about two months ago and had a killing in his family, and also reported documents being stolen. John, do you recall that you replaced Caesar Ponte with another person because he had difficulty handling vendors."

John thought for a moment and responded, "Yes, I recall the problem. I know the people in Brazil, and if that is the next place to be hit, I think I need to go to Rio de Janeiro. If we can get to Rio before they try to kill the leaders of the Medical Project, then maybe we can capture the killers before they strike and find out who is behind all the killings. What do you think, Jim?"

"I was thinking the same thing. Even though you had to remove Caesar from his job, you and he are still good friends. Maybe he may know who is behind these killings. He knows about everything that is going on in Brazil. He also really likes the Medical Project. Also, you speak a little Portuguese."

Kate had a worried look and said, "I am worried about John going on this trip. As you recall, there are a lot of criminal elements existing in Brazil. If he goes, you need to ensure proper security does exist. What is the plan to ensure we have sufficient security, Jim?"

"I plan to send Bill Collins with John throughout the whole trip. I will also arrange to have the US Ambassador to Brazil use his security when John is in Brazil. Additionally, I will arrange to have the Ambassador meet them at the airport with extra security."

John looked at Kate and said, "It will be OK. I think I will take one database person with me on this trip. The people in Brazil were doing some good work on databases before we left the project. Also, since Brazil was ahead of others in the database area, the database person can bring back a template that can be used when we restart the project.

Jeff Simpson is the best database person. We planned on using him to lead in putting the overall template together leading the database effort worldwide. Jeff worked on the project with you and me when we started and has spent five months in Rio de Janeiro. I also understand he is working with you on another project, Jim. Can we put him back on this project? We need to get to Jeff and Bill now so they can get ready for the trip. I think I have to leave tonight. I do not want to delay getting this solved. What do you guys think?"

Jim responded, "Sure, we will put him back on this project."

Kate also responded to Jim, "I agree that we better move fast before they eliminate everyone left working on this project. Be careful, John."

"I will call you from the airport, Kate. Let me get Bill on the walkie-talkie so he can go home and pack. I will have another guard take me home to pack. Jim, can you tell Jeff we will need him on this trip and to meet me at the airport?"

"Will do, John. Have a safe trip."

Jeff is married and has a 14-year-old daughter. He was a person that really knew computers and how to handle big projects. He can also handle difficult situations since he was a West Point graduate and an officer in the service.

John hugged and kissed Kate and told her he would call her. He then left the building and was met by a bodyguard at the door. He then got into the car with the guard and headed to his house.

When John got to the house, the guard inspected the house before John went in. The guard opened the door and told John, "It is OK to come in."

John said, "Thank you, do you want anything to eat or drink?" "No, thank you."

He then proceeded to the bedroom and packed a small bag he could carry on the plane. After packing and changing into some clothes that were more comfortable, he came out of his bedroom and said to the guard, "I am ready to go." They then both went to the car and got in.

On the way to the airport, John called Katelin on his cell phone and said, "Katelin, I am heading off the Rio de Janeiro and just wanted to make sure you are ok."

"I am fine, Daddy. Thank you for calling. I will make sure Mom is OK when you are gone."

"Thank you, Katelin. I will try to give you a call from Rio de Janeiro. I love you."

The car pulled up to the airport, and the guard said to the car driver, "Please wait for me. I will be back as soon as I can ensure the other guard is here."

They walked into the airport and up to the ticket counter. They saw Bill and Jeff at the ticket counter. Bill waved at John, and John walked over to Bill and Jeff and said, "I appreciate you guys coming on such short notice. It is important that we find out who is trying to stop the project and also get this project started."

After the guard that brought John saw that everything was ok, he said goodbye to everyone and went back out to the car.

Everyone then got their tickets and headed off to the airport lounge to wait for boarding. At the lounge, everyone got something to drink and some snacks and sat down. John then turned to Jeff and said, "We will discuss the database situation in more detail when we get to Brazil, but for now, I will say that I believe the database management will be the key to this project's success. We will need to input and access data within the database without delays. If there are delays, then people will not use the system. As you know, the amount of data will be huge since it will contain information on almost everyone and also proper things to do to cure any illness."

Jeff responded, "John, I understand the problem. The computers and storage devices we have today should not be a problem. Five years ago, it would have been impossible to do this project, but now with most doctors on the Internet and computer storage device enhancements, we will be able to make this happen."

On the flight, Bill was sitting next to John, and while they were eating their meals, Bill asked, "John, how do like the people you have in Brazil or Hong Kong?"

"Kate and I were in Brazil for about two years and five months ago trying to solve some problems that were happening in that country. We were in Rio de Janeiro, staying at one of the hotels on the Ipanema beach. It is one of the most beautiful cities in the world, and there is a beautiful six-mile run along the beach from Ipanema to Copacabana.

The only problem was that the people assigned the project in Brazil were subcontracting work out to the wrong people, and there were overruns in the budget. The people running the project had to be replaced because they did not know how to manage vendors.

We also spent about one month in Hong Kong about three years ago trying to get things set up throughout the smaller countries in Asia. During some of the meetings, they found that people in Hong Kong were giving information to people in other countries that were not part of the twenty countries working on the project. We decided not to stop this since this really helps people, but we could not support the other countries. The idea was that once we got the twenty countries active, we would then bring on other countries and it would be easy to bring them on once everything was debugged.

Now that Hong Kong as become a part of China, then we can have the people in Hong Kong lead all of China. Then we can have Singapore be the country that can lead all the smaller countries in Asia.

Bill responded, "Let's plan on doing that run along the beach when we are there. For now, we better get some sleep."

JOHN'S TRIP TO RIO DE JANEIRO

They arrived at the airport in Rio at about seven in the morning the next day. In Brazil, there is a VISA required, so John, Bill, and Jeff all went through customs and were on their way down to get Bill's luggage. They were all waiting for Bill's luggage when Bill asked Jeff and John, "How do you guys feel? I know that after one of these flights, I am usually tired because you only get about five hours sleep on that flight if you are lucky."

Jeff responded, "That's about how many hours sleep I got, but I am ready to go."

John responded, "That is the way I feel also, but we will make up that sleep tonight. Bill, what is our plan for getting to the guards and cars that will take us to the city?"

Bill responded, "Once we go through customs, there is a sliding door that opens automatically as you go out into the main portion of the airport. I am giving you each a walkie-talkie. I will call you when it is clear to come through the sliding glass doors and into the main portion of the airport. You will be safe in this area of the airport."

Bill then went through the door to the main portion of the airport. As he exited, a person was holding a sign with his name on it. He responded to the person holding the sign, "That's me. The other two people are waiting for me to tell them when to come out. Who are you?"

"I am Franco, the security guard from the ambassador's office. The ambassador and his personal security guard are in the ambassador's car. We also have a van and police car escorting us. The three of you can go to the hotel and then to the agency after you shower and change clothes."

Bill responded, "Rather than the three of us going into the same car, I would like to have John go with the Ambassador and his security guard in the car. That will also allow them to talk on the way to the city. I will go in the van. There will be another person traveling in the van with us. The police car can lead the way, and we will follow the ambassador's car in the van. Franco, does that sound OK with you?

"That sounds good. I will call the three cars and then let you know when they are at the airport's front door.

Once the police car, the ambassador's car, and the van arrived at the front door of the airport door, Franco ran up to Bill and said, "The cars are ready."

Bill called John on the walkie-talkie and said, "John, the transportation is ready. You will be with the ambassador, and Jeff and I will be in the van."

At that moment, John and Jeff came through the door, and Bill said, "OK, let's go." The security guards, Jeff and John, all made their way to the car and van.

Once they were in the car and van, the police car led the way, and the ambassador's car followed and then the van. They started to make their way from the airport to the city of Rio. It is about a one-hour ride if there is not too much traffic. John was briefing the ambassador as they followed the police car.

About fifteen minutes from the airport, there is a favella. It is another name for a slum area or a shantytown. They are located all over Brazil, and going into the area is risky. No one goes into those areas except people living there. Even the police do not like to go in there. The world's largest favella is right outside Rio de Janeiro, with a population of over three hundred thousand. The favella just outside the airport has about a hundred thousand people.

John continued to brief the ambassador as they proceeded down a four-lane divided highway. Then all of a sudden, the police car, ambassador's car, and van stopped. It looked like there was a traffic jam up ahead. John asked the driver, "What seems to be holding things up."

"I do not know, but one of the police officers has gotten out of the car and is walking forward to where the traffic is stopped."

John then got Bill on the walkie-talkie, "Bill, can you see anything from the van?"

"No, I can't. It just seems like a big traffic jam. There seem to be some dump trucks that may have gotten into an accident. Wait a second. Oh my God, there are people with guns coming out of the trucks and running towards us. They just shot a police officer, and the police engaged them in a gun battle. John, see if you can have the car driver cut across the large grass area separating traffic coming into the airport and leaving the airport. We will make room for you to back up, turn the car, and cut across the grass area. We will follow you to protect your backside."

John then gave instructions to the ambassador's driver to go across the grass area. John looked out the window as the car turned, and he quickly updated the ambassador by saying, "It looks like people from the favellas are going from car to car stealing and killing people. There are about fifty cars stopped in front of us on the highway and it looks like a couple of trucks blocking the road up front and about twenty cars blocking us from behind."

Bill, the ambassador's guard, and Franco all pulled their guns and started firing at the people as they approached the car and van. John, Jeff, and the ambassador did not carry guns but everyone else was carrying a gun. There were two more police officers that got out of the police car, and they were firing their guns.

As the robbers got closer to the van and car, John noticed that they were yelling out his name. At that point, Bill yelled out, "They are here to get John. Hurry and get the ambassador's car across the grass area."

The island was a grassy area that was about thirty yards across, so it would be difficult to cross. As they started to pull across the island, the people with machine guns began to open fire on the car. The van had not started across the island yet. The security guards in the van and car began firing back at the people with the machine guns. At that point, the tires in the car were fired on and went flat. The engine also exploded, and the car came to a stop.

John yelled to Bill, "The driver and the ambassador's guard are dead. The ambassador is wounded. We are coming to the van. Open the side door." John grabbed the guard's gun, carried the ambassador on his back, and began running toward the van and shooting as he ran.

As John approached the van, he noticed the driver and guard were lying dead outside the van, and John said, "Bill lay the ambassador down in the back of the van. Oh my god, Jeff, you are also shot. Stay in the back with the ambassador and hold on. We are going across this island. We are getting out of here."

The people from the favella were still moving closer as they ran between the cars. John then got in the driver's seat. The van was running, but he needed room to turn toward the island, so he banged into the car behind him, pushed it back, and then pulled out quickly so he could drive across the island. Before John started across the island, he yelled out to Bill, "Get that machine gun by those dead police officers and get in the van. We are cutting across the island."

Bill grabbed the gun from the dead police officer and then yelled out to John, "I got the gun. John, let's go!" Bill kept firing and kept the favella people pinned down as John cut across the island.

As they got halfway across the grassy area, John yelled, "Two cars are coming after us. See if you can hit their tires, Bill."

Bill yelled back to John, "Look up, John! We have been rescued." Two helicopters were heading toward the cars and also the favella people.

The helicopters fired their guns at the cars. Both cars exploded. Then the helicopters started firing at the favella people. After a few minutes, the favella people started running back to the favella area.

John was able to make it to the other side of the road and began going the wrong way against traffic but got ahead of the trucks blocking the street and then cut back across the island, so he was again going with traffic.

Four police cars were waiting on the other side. They then began to escort them back into the city with two police cars in front, two in the rear, and two helicopters above as they went straight to a hospital in Rio. John pulled the van right up to the door of the hospital. One of the police cars had pulled ahead of them when they were one mile from the hospital and had everyone waiting for their arrival. John went to the emergency entrance, jumped out of the van, and said, "We have two injured people here that need your help. One of them is the US Ambassador."

One of the doctors said, "The police told us about what happened, and we have two stretchers. We will be getting the injured people to the operating room immediately. We will need you to wait in the waiting room area."

About twenty minutes later, a nurse came out and said, "They are both in the operating room."

John said, "Has anyone contacted the wives of the injured people?"

The nurse said, "Yes, and your government agency has contacted both wives, and they understand the situation." It is not serious, but we will keep them in the hospital overnight."

While John was waiting at the hospital, he called Jim and said, "Jim, I just wanted to let you know that there was an attempt made on our lives when we were going from the airport to Rio. I am OK, and so is Bill, but Jeff and the US Ambassador are being operated on now. The doctor believes they will be OK. We were lucky. There were several Brazil Police Officers killed. They need to increase the security here, and Bill is looking into making that happen. I plan to stay at the hospital until the operations have been completed, and then I will head off to the hotel."

"Thank God that you are OK. I will make sure that the head of security gives Bill whatever he needs. Kate is here with me. I will put her on the line."

"Hello Kate, please don't worry. I am OK, and security will be increased. I am concerned that there is a leak in the agency since they knew about my arrival. I will call you tonight from the hotel. You better call Katelin and let her know I am OK. Also, you should call Bill's wife and let her know that Bill was great and he is OK. Jeff's wife has been contacted. He is in surgery and should be ok, but you or Jim may want to call her also. I noticed that there are people from the press here, and this may make the news."

As soon as John hung up, Jim began checking things back at his end concerning the leak. He also made a call to Jeff's wife. Kate called Katelin at work and told her, "Katelin, your dad is OK, but some people in Brazil were trying to kill him. The US Ambassador and Jeff Simson were injured. Please don't worry if you see anything on the news."

"Mom, just before you called somebody mentioned to me that it was just coming on the news. They did not mention Daddy's name, but they did mention the US Ambassador was injured and also talked a little about the medical project. What is going on?"

"We knew it would be difficult at the start of the project, but we never expected this. We will be prepared the next time something like this happens. I just talked with Dad, and he is OK."

"OK, Mom, I will talk with you tonight. Thanks for calling. I feel a lot better. Please be careful."

Kate then picked up the phone and called Bills wife and let her know Bill was OK and told her not to worry.

Back in Rio, John was still in the waiting room and went over to the couch and sat down and picked up a Brazil magazine, and began reading it. After a while, he got up and went over to the nurse at the waiting room desk and asked in Portuguese, "Any information on the US Ambassador and Jeff Simson?"

"Nothing yet, but the doctor will come out and speak with you as soon as we have any information. He knows you are waiting."

Just then, Bill came in the emergency entrance door. He had been talking with the police and also people from the agency. Bill said to

John, "I have things set up with the police and our agency. We will be more prepared if they should try this again."

John responded, "That is great news. I had Jim call your wife and let her know what happened and that you are OK. You may want to call her yourself right now to let her know you are OK."

"Thanks, John, that is a good idea."

Bill went over to the phone in the waiting room and called his wife, letting her know the whole story and not to worry. After the call, Bill sat on the couch across from John. During that time, the Ambassador's wife came into the waiting room. Everyone introduced themselves, and then they all waited for about two hours.

Then the doctors came out to the waiting room and calmly said to John and the Ambassadors wife, "They both came through the operation OK. I had to remove a bullet from each of their shoulders. They lost a lot of blood, and their arms will be in a sling for a couple of days. A little lower, and the bullets would have hit their hearts. I want to keep them in the hospital for a day before they go home. I will let the ambassador's wife see him for five minutes."

John said, "I would like to see both of them before I go. Do you think it would be OK for me to see them for five minutes also?"

"Yes, you can both go in and see them, but I would like them to sleep through the night, so just take five minutes and do not excite them."

They followed the doctor to the elevator and then up to the private rooms where the US Ambassador and Jeff were located. Each had their own private rooms, which were located next to each other. There were two guards outside their door, plus a guard at the elevator. All had machine guns.

The ambassador's wife went into the ambassador's room, so John went to talk with Jeff. When John walked in, there was a chair beside the bed, so John sat down in the chair and said, "Jeff, I never thought they would do something like this. Kate has called your wife to let her know things were OK. How do you feel?"

"Don't worry, John, I feel fine. I also called her before the operation.

I told her I was OK and not to worry."

"Do you think they will let me call my wife from here?"

John picked up the phone and got an outside line and used his calling card to get through to his wife, and said, "Here it is, Jeff, the phone is ringing."

As soon as Jeff got his wife on the line, John, thought it would be best to leave the room and let them talk in private, so he said, "Tell her I said hello. I will leave you two to talk alone. I will see you tomorrow."

As John was walking out of the room, Jeff said, "John thank you for coming by and also for saving my life. See you tomorrow."

John then went into the ambassador's room. His wife was sitting in the chair beside his bed. John said, "Mr. Ambassador, how are you feeling?"

"I am OK. How is Jeff doing?"

"Jeff is doing fine. I just hooked him up with his wife."

"John, I would like to see you as soon as I get out of this hospital. I want to find the people who are responsible for this."

"I understand, Mr. Ambassador. I will be focused on getting the people responsible for this. I will talk with you tomorrow. Please get some rest."

"John, another thing, I want to thank you for saving my life."

"See you tomorrow, Mr. Ambassador."

The ambassador's wife got out of her chair and had a tear in her eye and gave John a hug and a kiss on the cheek, and said, "Thank you for saving my husband's life."

John then went down to the waiting room area where Bill was waiting for him. Bill looked at John and said, "It's been a long day. How are you feeling."

John responded, "It has been a long day. Let's get to the hotel and get some rest."

When John and Bill left the hospital, it was seven and just getting dark outside. There was a police car escort and also a security guard that went with them in the car. All were heavily armed. The police car stayed outside the hotel, and one of the bodyguards went into the hotel with Bill and John. They both checked into the hotel, and John told the manager, "Jeff Simson will not be checking in tonight but will be coming tomorrow night."

The manager responded, "I understand. We were informed, and everything that has happened has been on the TV, including the complete story about what you are trying to do to improve the medical industry around the world.

We are very sorry this has happened in our country. Here are several drink coupons you both can use while you are staying at the hotel. We have upgraded you to suites overlooking the beach. Our bellman will take your suitcases to your rooms."

John looked at the manager, and he saw that he felt bad about what had happened, so he responded, "This has nothing to do with your country it is just a few people that are trying to stop something that would benefit the world. We will find the people who killed the police and will move ahead with the project. Thank you for your help."

Before getting in the elevator, John asked Bill, "Do you want to sit down for a minute to have a drink? I think I am skipping dinner tonight."

Bill responded, "Yes, I can use a drink. The Brazil police will be doing the guarding tonight."

Bill and John went into a small bar containing several tables and chairs with a piano player. The guard sat at a table close to their table. John looked Bill directly in the eye with an upset look on his face and said, "Whoever is trying to stop the Medical Project is pretty smart and will not let this one mistake stop them. Since this is one of their first misses, they will try again—even harder. We should be prepared for another hit."

Bill responded, "We are ready for them, John. We will go through the details tomorrow. What time do you want to wake up tomorrow?"

"Since we are getting to bed early, I will try to wake up at six and run on the treadmill. We have a breakfast meeting with Juan Carlos at eight in the hotel's breakfast room, and then we can go to the office afterward."

"That sounds like a plan. I will make sure security is ready, and I will run with you in the morning."

After they finished their drinks, they got in the elevator and went to their rooms. The rooms were next to each other, and there was a guard outside their door. When John got into the room, he remembered that it was the same room that he and his wife were in when they were working on the project in Rio. He then sat down on his bed and picked up the phone and called Kate, and said, "Hello, my love. I am in my hotel room and ready to go to bed. Please don't worry. It is very safe, plus I have bodyguards all over the place."

"John, please take care of yourself and don't take any chances. I talked with Katelin, and she said she saw something on the news, but I told her you were OK and not to worry.

Kate, I got our old room. It overlooks the ocean. It brings back great memories. I miss you and love you."

"I miss you too. Please get some rest, and I will talk with you tomorrow."

That night John had a dream that he had once before while in Ipanema. One of the biggest favellas in the world was located on a hill about 3 miles from Ipanema. You could see the shacks from his hotel window. They look like little dots along the hillside. This was the favella that had over 300,000 people.

His dream has the people in the favella invading the city and going door to door in the hotel, killing people. He always wakes up when they come to his door. This time when he woke up, he let out a yell. One of the guards sitting outside his room opened the door with an extra key and immediately came into the room and turned on the light. The other guard stood in the doorway so he would have a view of the room and also the hall outside the room. John woke up in a sweat and told them, "Sorry, it was just a bad dream."

"One of the guards looked John in the eye and, with a serious look, said, "You deserve to have bad dreams based on the day you just had.

Try to get some rest." He then turned off the light, shut the door, and locked it.

John always had the capability of going to sleep right after he woke up at night, and as soon as his head hit the pillow, he was asleep again.

◆

Meetings with Brazil Medical Project Leaders

The next morning John woke up at six and called the hospital and found out that the ambassador and Jeff were OK and were still scheduled to be checked out of the hospital today. John then put on his running outfit and started the coffee machine inside his room.

John then looked outside his door, and there was Bill, two guards, and another person, so John looked surprised and said, OK, Bill, let's go exercise. Who is your friend?"

"He is our driver. I believe you know the other two guys."

John then said, "We are going to run on the treadmill today. I will be ready in about 10 minutes. I am making some coffee. Does anyone want any coffee? "

Bill responded, "We just had a cup. I think we are set."

After John had his coffee, he opened the door and stepped out into the hall. Bill was there with the two guards. John said, "I am ready, Bill. Are you ready to do some running?"

"I think I had enough exercise yesterday, so I will skip my run today and just do some weights when you run."

"OK, we will need to go to the top floor. That is where the exercise room is located." The two guards, Bill and John, then went over to the elevator to go to the top floor. When you get off the elevator and go to the right, you will see the breakfast area, and when you go to the left, you will enter the exercise room.

John said as they got off the elevator, "I wish we were going to the right to have breakfast but let's get in our exercise and go to the left."

John started running on the treadmill, and Bill began lifting weights. One of the guards stayed in the exercise room with them, and the other stayed outside. They were the only ones in the room. John pointed to the street below and said, "Tomorrow morning, we need to exercise out there. It is beautiful, and there are a lot of people walking and running along the pathway beside the beach."

Bill looked at the police officer and said, "Let's set everything up so it will be safe if we run outside around the same time." The police officer nodded to affirm that things would be set up.

John, with a look of concern, said, "If this is any trouble, then we can run inside again."

The police officer said, "Don't worry, you will be safe. If you want to run outside tomorrow, it will be safe."

John stopped his run after about six miles, then got off the treadmill and said, "I am glad this is over. We worked all this weight off now. Let's have fun putting it back on.

Bill, we better get back to our rooms and get ready for work. Don't forget we have a breakfast meeting set up with Juan Carlos, the person who is running the Medical Project here in Brazil. I believe he is going to meet with us up here in the breakfast room at about seven forty-five. We will probably be heading off to work around nine."

Juan Carlos was married, had two children, spoke several languages, was very good at managing big projects and was a runner. John and Juan Carlos used to run every morning when they worked on getting the project back on track. This was when John lived in a hotel for a while in Rio de Janeiro.

John and Bill then went back to their rooms, followed by the two guards. After about a half-hour, John and Bill came out of their rooms at about the same time and headed to breakfast. The breakfast room was where Kate and John used to have breakfast every day when they were in Brazil. On the top floor of the hotel, there was a swimming pool. The restaurant was half indoors and half outdoors, with tables and chairs all around the pool. There was a beautiful view of the ocean and people exercising along the beach, which could be seen from all the seats in the restaurant.

As John entered the breakfast room, he noticed that Juan Carlos was not there, so he told Bill, "Well, it looks like Juan Carlos is not here. Let's grab a table, and order coffee, and wait for him." They sat at a table for four overlooking the beach and twin peak mountains. John had a smile on his face and was admiring the view while he told Bill, "Isn't this beautiful?" He pointed to the buffet, saying, "The buffet has the greatest fruit in the world, plus you can order from the menu if you like." Then John pointed to two mountains and said, "The twin peak mountains over there are called the brothers by the people in Rio. The reason that the peaks were called the brothers was that they were so close."

Just then, Juan Carlos walked into the room with another person, walked over to where John was sitting, and said, "John, my friend." John stood up and said, "Juan Carlos, my friend." They both hugged each other, which was a custom in Brazil. As they parted, John said, "How are you doing?"

"I am fine now. I want to thank you for saving my life. If you did not call the agency and let them know about what was happening, then I would not have this bodyguard and other security. I would probably be dead."

"Juan Carlos, the important thing right now is to find out who is doing these killings, but before we get into that discussion, let's get some breakfast. I know you know how the buffet works since we ate here many times."

They all got their breakfast, and Bill and the other security guard moved to another table closer to the door so they could have a good view of the room and people coming into the restaurant. After John and Juan Carlos were finished with breakfast, John showed Juan Carlos a list of names and said, "Look at this list of names of possible people that could be responsible for all the problems here in Brazil. I have put Caesar Ponte at the top of the list. I like Caesar, and he is a good friend. He was in your position when I came here. I had to remove him because he did not know how to handle vendors. If he is not the one doing it, then he may know who is responsible for the raid on the Ambassador and me. He may even know who could be responsible for all the killing that is going on in the Medical Project. Getting to Caesar would not be easy. Caesar could be any place in Brazil."

"I agree, John. We need to find Caesar. I do have some ideas about where he can be. I agree with you, and if he did not do it, he should know who did since he is on top of everything in Brazil. Also, if he did not do anything, he should be easy to find out who is responsible for all the problems."

"Juan Carlos, it looks like we are both done with breakfast. Should we get to the agency?"

"Yes, let's go. I will ride with you in your car."

As John got up, he took one more long view of the beach and mountains. It was beautiful. He and Juan Carlos walked to the elevators with two police officers in front of them and Bill and Juan Carlos's security guard behind them. When they reached the lobby floor, there were two more police officers in the elevator. They all walked out the door. The car was waiting. John, Juan Carlos, Bill, and Juan Carlos's security guard got in. One police car was in front and the other was behind the car.

John and Juan Carlos were sitting in the car next to each other.

John was looking out the window and told Juan Carlos, "The offices are on the other side of the city, and I really like this ride. This ride along the Ipanema and Copacabana beach is so relaxing. All along the way, you see people playing all kinds of games. Then as you approach the tunnel leading to the other side and look up to your left, you see the Christ Statue located on top of one of the highest mountains in Rio in a city called Corcovado. It is one of the best rides in the world."

"I agree with you, John; it has the ocean, the sand, and beautiful people."

"I am not sure about beautiful people. It seems like there are people in these nylon bathing suits that probably should be in boxer-type bathing suits. They don't seem to care how they look in their suits."

"You are right; the people in Rio believe that all bodies are beautiful."

"I am not so sure of that, Juan Carlos. There are an awful lot of plastic surgeons in Rio."

One of the things that John noticed when he approached the agency is that the US Ambassador, Jim, and Bill did a good job with the Brazilian government in getting proper security in place based on what happened the day before.

Everyone got out of the car, and there was a Brazil Police Officer at the entrance that greeted them at the door. The Brazil Police Officer said, "My name is Fabio Sotos. I am the person that is assigned to work with Bill and also take over the guarding Juan Carlos."

Fabio knew Juan Carlos so when Fabio caught Juan Carlos's eye, they both hugged, and Fabio said, "It is great to see you again, my friend. I am the new officer that will be assigned to guard you and assist in this effort."

Fabio was one of the elite police officers in Brazil that had some training in the US. He was from Rio de Janeiro and spoke English very well and, of course, Portuguese. He was a good-looking person and thirty-four years old, 6 ft, and 180 lb.

Fabio and Bill led everyone into the building. Once inside, Juan Carlos took us to an area that was set aside for us to work. Fabio and two other police officers accompanied us to our offices. The local police were involved because once we found Caesar, we would need them to help us get to Caesar. John asked Fabio, "Fabio can you use some of the resources you have in the police department to help us locate Caesar. I will use the connection we have at the agency. Let's get back together in two hours and see where we are."

John, Bill, Fabio, and Juan Carlos then walked over to some offices next to the office Fabio was in, and John said to Juan Carlos, "I am going to plug in my PC and link up with the computer systems in the US and see if they have any information for us or if they were able to trace where Caesar was last located and also get an address for some of his family members that were located in Rio." Bill stayed with John in his office, and the others went to other offices.

Juan Carlos responded, "My office is right next to this one. I will call some people in human resources since Caesar did work for the agency here in Rio. I will also see if they can find where Caesar banks and what credit card he uses. His records should show who in his family was the emergency contact." Fabio followed Juan Carlos to his office and stayed with him.

Everyone was working through their sources to find where Caesar was located, and after two hours, Juan Carlos came into John's office and said, "John, it has been two hours, and can we all get together in your office?

"Yes, I am ready."

Juan Carlos then went to get the police so he could bring them into John's office. A few minutes later, everyone showed up in John's office and sat down. John was working on his computer and looked over and saw everyone was ready, so he said, "OK, I have a possible address where Caesar could be. Juan Carlos, did you get an address also?"

"Yes, I did."

"OK, let's compare them, and hopefully, they are the same."

John had his written down on a piece of paper, and so did Juan Carlos. They both laid their papers down on the table, and John, with great enthusiasm, said, "Great, it is a match. Now Fabio, if we go to this address, will you be able to supply security and people just in case we need to force Caesar to see us."

"Yes, I can. We will be ready to go in thirty minutes."

John then said, "OK, guys, I think we have confirmed where Caesar is now living. Let's go talk with him. Everyone close down what they are doing, and we will meet back here in about thirty minutes and leave."

In about thirty minutes they all met in John's office and then left the agency and started going to Caesar's home. Waiting for them as they exited the building was a car and five cars full of Brazil Police.

Juan Carlos, Fabio, John, and Bill were all in the car, and there were three police cars in front of them and two police cars following them. All the police were heavily armed. As they headed north out of Rio, Juan Carlos pointed out the window and said, "This is a small section of the rain forest, and it is just north of the city of Rio de Janeiro. The houses in this area are mansions. Usually, the very rich live up here. John, do you have areas like this in the United States?"

"I have never seen areas like this. The dense forest makes it look lush and the houses are very big."

After about an hour, they reached the address where they thought Caesar was located. Altogether, about twenty people were armed, and if necessary, armed helicopters could be called in for support.

Caesar's house was surrounded by a ten-foot-high wall with a large wooden gate. It looked like the house was on a thirty-acre parcel of land. It had a swimming pool in front with a long winding driveway with trees on either side leading up to the house.

They rang the bell at the gate, and a voice came over the intercom saying, "Hello, who is there?"

John recognized Caesar's voice on the other end, so he responded, "Caesar, it is John Colombo. Can we talk with you for a moment?"

Caesar recognized John's voice and saw him and everyone else in the camera, "Hello John, how are you doing. It is great to hear your voice. You can come in with no, more than three other people because I do not want to frighten my family."

"OK, Caesar."

John decided to have Juan Carlos, Bill, and Fabio go in with him. John spoke to the speaker outside the gate and said, "Caesar, we are ready to come in." The large gate began to open slowly.

There was a long driveway, so they all got in a police car, which Fabio drove and proceeded down the driveway. Along the driveway, there were two heavily armed guards. As they approached the house, there was another armed guard. It was a huge single-story house surrounded by large trees. Directly in front of the house, there was a circular drive with a big fountain in the middle.

The house looked old, but based on the data we got from the computer, we knew it was not more than two years old. John then recalled Caesar telling him that a dream he had was to build a new house made from old houses located throughout Brazil. It looks like he fulfilled his dream.

They got out of the car, and Caesar met everyone at the door. He immediately walked up to John, gave him a big hug, and said, "It is so nice to see you again my friend. Please come in."

He led everyone into his den. Caesar was a doctor and had computer experience, making him ideal for this project. He was first picked for the project because of his background, but when it came to controlling vendors, he failed, and that is why he had to be replaced.

Once in the den, Caesar said, "John, I heard about the problem you had on the way into Rio from the airport. I also understand that people working on the project around the world are being killed."

John then said, "How do you know all these things, and did you have anything to do with these killings?

"John, I have a lot of connections in Rio. My family lives here. I also keep track of the project that Juan Carlos is now running. As you know, I am a doctor, in the business of saving lives, not killing people. I had nothing to do with any of these killings. I only found out about what happened by reading about it, watching television, and talking with people."

"I believe you, Caesar, but do you have any idea who could be behind all these killings?"

All the other people were sitting at a table, and Caesar got up and began to tell us a story. You could tell by the strain on his face that this was very difficult for him. He began by saying, "This is a difficult story for my wife and me to tell or think about. It started one night when I was at home with my wife and two sons. Some men had climbed over the wall around the house and then cut the alarm system and broke into the house. At that time, I did not have any guards. It also was one of the few weekends when my whole family was home. Usually, my sons are at college in the dorms or studying, but they were on break.

It was nine at night, and we were all sitting in the living room watching TV. Then without any warning, three heavily armed masked men came into the room from the side. They must have been experts because we did not hear a thing until they were in the room. They came at us from the side and asked us to raise our arms and move against the wall. We were stunned.

They asked for our guns, money, and any information we had on the Medical Project. They were specifically interested in a list of people that were involved in our project worldwide. They were all wearing ski masks.

One of my sons spoke up, telling them to get out of the house or they would get in trouble. They immediately shot him in front of us. The bullet was fired at his heart and killed him immediately. They wanted to let us know they meant business. Our son was in his first year of medical school with a great deal of promise. He was just a young boy, never thinking anything bad could happen to him. I do not know how many times I have told him that if someone has a gun or a knife and wants something, just give it to them and do not ask questions.

At that point, I told them to tell me again what they wanted, and I would get it for them. I told my wife and son to remain quiet and not say a word. Again, they repeated their request. I told them I would have to go to different rooms in order to get them what they wanted.

They told me that two people would go with me to get what they requested and one person would stay with my wife and son. I got them the one gun we had in the house. We also had $2000 and the Medical Project information they requested in a safe, which I gave them."

John asked Caesar, "Was this the list of people that were involved in the project around the world? Why did you hold on to the list after we let you go?"

"That was the list of key people we knew around the world. It was the list that you sent to key people on the project, which contained the names, responsibilities, and locations of all key people on the project. I kept it because these were people that were still corresponding with me and were my friends. Also, I was thinking of asking Juan Carlos about returning to the project. I knew the list was important and had it in the safe."

Juan Carlos then asked, "Did they leave after they got what they wanted?"

"Once they got everything they wanted, they left saying do not try to come after us, or you will all die. I contacted the police on my cell phone since the other phone lines were cut. The police arrived within an hour and took down all the information I had on the killing and robbery. They tried to find information on these people, but since they wore masks and had gloves, any hope of finding these people was almost impossible. We never heard anything from the police after that day. At that time, we did not link the killings around the world to my robbery."

John looked at Fabio and asked, "Do you have any record of this tragedy."

"Yes, we do, but we could not locate the killer and did not pursue it after one month."

John then said, "Caesar, I am so sorry for your loss. If you help us, we will find your son's killers. If Juan Carlos is OK with you coming back, then we would like you to consider coming back to the project to work for Juan Carlos. We are going to restart this project worldwide as soon as we can find who is responsible for all this killing."

Juan Carlos responded, "It would be great to have Caesar back on the project."

"I appreciate the faith you have in me and also the second chance. I do want to help find the killers of my son, and I also want to help with the project. You can count on me."

John then said, "OK, let's strategize who in Brazil could be trying to kill people associated with this project. Once we find that person, then we should be able to find your son's killers."

Caesar then said, "There are about five mob people that have close ties with people in the favellas. These people were responsible for a great deal of crime in Brazil. The police and I know who these people are, but we need to link the one mob boss in Brazil with the person in the US that is trying to stop the Medical Project worldwide."

John said, "Why do you think the overall leader for this is in the US?"

Juan Carlos responded, "The mob people in Brazil are not strong enough to be doing this around the world, and they had nothing to gain since they were not in the medical business. It was clear that they were being paid to make an effort in Brazil come to an end."

Caesar also said, "I agree. I am getting the same input from people I know."

John then said, "OK, then let's go down two paths. I will determine who the leader of the worldwide effort is, and at the same time, we will start gathering the evidence to find out who in Brazil is being paid off by that person."

Fabio then said, "John, if you can work with us on Friday, then we can put a plan together. We will work together in finding the mob leader in Brazil responsible for the problem, and after we find him, we will get the people that work for him and then determine his boss."

John responded, "OK, let me see, it is now Wednesday night, and I believe it will take a couple of more days to get everything lined up. Jeff and I will plan to stay in Rio de Janeiro over the weekend and leave Monday."

Fabio then said with great enthusiasm, "Thank you, John. If you can do that, then I am sure we will find the mob boss and get to the bottom of all of this. Caesar, thank you also for all the help you have given us. Is there anything we can do for you?"

Caesar responded, "Yes, just one thing. Find the killers of my son."

When they left, John hugged Caesar and kissed his wife on the cheek, and said, "I am so sorry about the loss of your son. I know he will never be forgotten. You have my word; we will find the killers."

Caesar's wife turned to John with a tear in her eye and responded, "Thank you, please find these monsters. I want you to keep this Saint Christopher metal my son used to wear. It will keep you safe. These people are very dangerous."

Then Caesar turned toward Juan Carlos and said, "Juan Carlos, I will be at work as soon as I can divert some of my patients."

Juan Carlos responded, "OK, Caesar would you mind if I leave a few police officers here to guard you and your family?"

Caesar had a sign of appreciation on his face when he said, "Thank you."

John and the others got back into the police car and headed back to the gate. When they got to the gate, Juan Carlos said to John, "I live about five miles from here, so I will have a police car take me home."

John responded, "OK, this was a good day. I will see you in the office tomorrow morning around nine."

Fabio said, "I will say goodbye for today, John, and will also take one police car and head home. The other three police cars will escort you back into the city, and some of these men will stay with you at the hotel."

John responded, "Thank you for making this happen today, Fabio. Please let your officers know we need to go to the hospital to pick up Jeff Simson, and then we will be going to the hotel. Also, can you have someone call the hospital and give a message to Jeff, letting him know that we will be there in about an hour?

"No problem, I will let the police know to escort you to both places and contact the hospital."

John and Bill then got into the car. The car driver turned to John and said, "First, we will go to the hospital and then to the hotel." A great deal of the time, things get repeated when English is not the native language to ensure everyone understands.

Bill responded, "Yes, that is right."

The car started moving through the rainforest, and John turned to Bill, pointed to the forest outside the window, and said, "Isn't this a beautiful area?"

"This is beautiful. I have never seen so many bushes and trees. Just an hour from here, and there are beaches and sand."

John switched the subject and asked Bill, "I would like to get to the agency at nine tomorrow morning. Can we run along the beach tomorrow morning?"

"I believe we need to run on the treadmill tomorrow. I think it is too dangerous to run outside now. Let me put some plans in place so we can run outside on Saturday."

For the remainder of the ride, Bill and John just looked out the window and dozed off now and then. After about an hour, the car pulled up to the hospital.

John got out of the car with Bill. Two police were in front of them, and two were behind them. They entered the hospital lobby and asked at the desk, "We are here to pick up Jeff Simson. Also, how is the US Ambassador?"

The administrator behind the desk said, "The US Ambassador just checked out about thirty minutes ago, and he is doing fine. Mr. Simson is in room 455."

Bill, John, and two police officers then got into the elevator and went to the room. When they got to the room, they noticed that Jeff had everything packed and was sitting in a chair looking at CNN on TV.

Jeff looked up and, with a smile, said, "Hey guys, you know, we are on CNN. Someone that was in a car during the ride into Rio from the airport had a movie camera, and they took pictures of everything that happened. John, I just wanted to thank you again for saving my life. I am ready to get out of here."

John responded, "How are you feeling?"

"I am feeling great. I just won't be able to use this arm for a while. I am ready to get some hotel food. Let's get out of here."

A nurse came into the room and said, "I must wheel you out of the hospital in the wheelchair."

Jeff got in the wheelchair and said, "I am ready."

They all went down to the lobby and then out the door to the car. The car had a police car in front and behind. They all started at the hotel and were there in about fifteen minutes.

They all stopped at the desk, and the person at the desk handed everyone a key. John then told Bill and Jeff, "This is probably a room service night. Jeff, this will give you a chance to get some more rest. We will go out for dinner tomorrow. I plan to go up to the exercise room tomorrow morning at six-thirty and then have breakfast at eight and leave for the agency at eight-thirty."

Bill responded, "OK, John, I will have the right security in place."

Jeff responded, "I will skip the exercise but meet you guys for breakfast."

They all went to their room, and after John showered, he decided to call his wife and give her a full update on what happened, so he picked up the phone and got her on the phone and said, "Kate, this was another exciting day. We talked to Caesar, and he offered to help us. He had a terrible tragedy. His son was killed by mob people due to this project. We told him we would find the killers, and he offered to help. His wife gave me this nice Saint Christopher medal that her son was wearing. I plan to get a chain and wear it around my neck until we find the killer."

"John, I really cannot believe all the tragedy that has happened around this project. We need to make sure we get the killers. We will start putting together a list of people who could have overall responsibility for all these killings. When do you think you can make it back to Washington?"

"Maybe I can leave Monday night if things go well."

"We will miss you. I hate it when you are gone over the weekend."

"I hate to be separated from you, Kate. I will call you every night. I love you. Take care."

"Bye, my love."

Dinner with Jeff and Bill

When John got up at around six, he started his coffee machine and got on his running clothes. He had some extra coffee, so he popped his head out the door and holding a cup of coffee said, "Does anyone want some coffee?" Everyone declined, so John returned to his room to finish his coffee.

A couple of minutes later, John went outside again, and Bill was waiting to go up to the exercise room. Two police officers stayed to guard Jeff and the rooms that Bill and John were in. Another two police officers followed Bill and John up to the exercise room.

They all went to the elevator. There was a guard at the elevator also. Bill and John got in the elevator and went up to the top floor. John was amazed by the view on the top floor of the hotel. The treadmill faced the beach and running path along the beach. He then commented to Bill, "This is magnificent view of the beautiful city. It is hard to believe there is so much crime in the city. Rio would be the best tourist place in the world if people did not have to worry about crime."

After exercising, everyone went back to their rooms, showered, and got dressed. At eight, Jeff, Bill, and John all met right outside John's room and went to the breakfast room together. They all went again to the top floor. Since there were two police at the table near the door, Bill decided to sit with John and Jeff. They all got their breakfast and sat down and observed the beautiful view.

When everyone finished breakfast, Bill said, "It is almost nine. We better head to the office. John, do you have any idea when you will be leaving the office tonight?"

"It may be a late night. I know we have flights for Sunday night, but, if possible, it would be great to get back home earlier." Jeff and Bill's eyes lit up. John knew everyone felt the same way he did about getting back with their families.

When you get out the door of the hotel, you immediately see the beach. There are always people walking along the beach. As they exited the door, there were two police cars to meet them, plus a big black SUV. As John got in the SUV with Bill and Jeff, he said, "Good job, Bill. I am not worried about security."

During the day, John and the team worked up a plan and got an agreement with the Brazil Police, a local agency, and the team back in Washington. Jim and Kate were briefed on what they found out at Caesar's house yesterday. Kate had already started working on the short list of people and companies that could benefit by having the project die.

At about seven that night, most of the work had been completed, and it was time to get back to the hotel. John mentioned to Jeff and Bill, "Do you feel like eating at a place where they have some great salads and desserts? It has a nice Brazilian atmosphere and we can walk there from the hotel. Bill, concerning security, if we can walk there from the hotel, and if we dress casually, no one will recognize us from the locals."

"I don't think so, John. I will make sure we have proper security at the restaurant and for our walk to the restaurant."

As they were leaving, they stopped by Juan Carlos's office to let him know they were going. Juan Carlos asked, "So what are you guys doing tonight?"

John responded, "I am going to take them to a nice Brazilian restaurant where we can get some real nice salads and desserts. It is only two blocks from the hotel so we can walk.

"You guys be careful and have a good dinner. See you tomorrow."

Bill, Jeff, and John went to the elevator and proceeded to the lobby.

When they got off the elevator, a police officer was waiting for them, and when they got to the outside door, there was a car and two police cars full of police. John looked at Bill and said, "I notice across the street there are several people with earplugs. Are those police undercover?"

Bill responded, "We are concerned that there will be another attempt on your life. If there is, we will be prepared. We want to catch some of these people alive and be able to question them."

The ride back to the hotel was uneventful, which is what John wanted. They all just looked out the window at the people and the activity going on at the beach. John pointed out the window and said, "Hey guys look at those people playing footvolley. It is like volleyball, but you can't use your hands. So, it is a mixture of soccer and volleyball. The people only use their feet, chest, and head to set up and volley the ball across the net."

After about thirty minutes stop-and-go traffic, they finally made it to the hotel. They all went to the desk to get their keys, and John said, "Should we meet outside our rooms in about fifteen minutes and then walk to the restaurant?"

Bill responded, "Sounds good."

They all went to their rooms to change into some casual clothes and met outside their rooms in the hall. They then went out the hotel's front door and started walking toward the restaurant.

There were two police in front and behind them, plus extra security if they needed it. All were dressed in plain clothes, so you did not know they were security.

It was twilight outside, and the walk along the beach was beautiful. John mentioned to Bill and Jeff, "This is a walk that Kate and I used to make several nights a week. Kate is a vegetarian, and this restaurant was ideal for her plus the walk is really nice."

Jeff was usually quiet, but he was so taken by everything around during the walk, and he said, "When you have the ocean, the stars, the beautiful old buildings, and some great friends, it is great. John, it is always good to work with you on projects. It seems like we are going all over the world, and we are always working on something that will make lives better."

John responded, "I bet you don't like all this danger."

"It will get better. I feel pretty safe now."

John pointed to the restaurant, saying, "OK, guys, we are here. I warned you it has a Brazilian atmosphere and is a place where local people go. You will not find too many tourists in this place. It will give us a chance to brush up on our Portuguese."

The place had two floors and was a very open type of restaurant. Two guards stayed outside, and two got a table near the door and within eye distance of John's table. Bill sat at the table with Jeff and John.

When they looked at the menu, Bill commented, "They have more than just salads at this restaurant. It looks like they have a bit of everything. What is this drink they call Guadana?"

John responded, "It is a drink made in Brazil and only sold in Brazil or stores where they sell Brazilian food in other countries. It is made from the berries from the rainforest. It is similar to our Cola, except it has a berry taste."

John looked at Jeff and switched subjects saying, "Jeff, you need to work with Juan Carlos to understand how we can take what he has done and incorporate it into a worldwide project. Then bring that information back to Kate, who is putting together an overall template."

Jeff responded, "In talking with Kate, she mentioned what she would need from me. I will try to see how big the databases need to be to hold all the information needed. Also, I need to check and make sure that people all over the world can use the data."

The databases containing all the medical information will be one of the biggest problems on this project, and you are our database expert, so you're focused on the right things.

If we can get this right, then we will be able to determine if there is more than the normal number of people dying of cancer because of some manufacturing facility polluting a water supply or air supply. These types of problems will be solved before they spread to hundreds of families. This also can shortcut legal battles in courts because we can make it a law that if cancer exceeds a certain limit and it is because of a manufacturing plant, then it can be shut down immediately. The Medical Project will contain all the facts necessary. You will need to write the efficient programs so that people can get to the data and also input the data easily and with little delay."

Jeff responded, "Thanks for the input Sometimes when you are so engrossed in how to technically make it happen, you lose sight of the big picture and what are the other effects of this project."

The waitress came by and asked for our order. She was impressed by Bill's Portuguese. After she took our order, John said to Bill, "You have been practicing your Portuguese, I see."

"I do what you taught me how to do, John. Right before I know I am going to a foreign country, I get out the language tapes and practice the language."

"John, I have not had a chance to ask you about your daughter. How is she doing?"

"She is doing great. The doctors have said that all of the cancer is gone. The only problem now is to make sure it does not pop up anywhere else in your body. They say if it stays away for five years, then there is a good chance it is gone forever. So, we have our fingers crossed."

"That sounds great."

John asked Jeff, "How is your family doing?"

"They're doing great. These trips are always hard on the family. It seems like this element of danger makes it a lot worst, but they realize what we are doing, so they all understand and are behind us."

As dinner was coming to an end, John said, "Bill, are we going to run along the beach tomorrow morning at six-thirty?"

"Sounds good to me. I have security aware of what we plan to do, so it should be safe. They said they will be with us all along the run."

Bill asked Jeff, "Jeff are you going to sleep in tomorrow morning?"
"Yes, I think I will sleep in but wake me if you need me for anything."

"We definitely will go to a good Brazilian restaurant tomorrow night. We will take in a Brazilian barbeque. So, don't eat too much meat. You will get enough meat for a month. I will call you sometime in the afternoon."

Everyone walked back to the hotel. As they went to their room, two guards stood outside the hotel, and two guards were outside their rooms. Things were secure.

EXCITEMENT ON THE BEACH

John woke up at about six, started up his coffee machine, put on his running clothes, stuck his head out the door, and said, "Do you guys want some coffee?"

"No, we just had breakfast."

"You better wake up Bill and let him know I will meet him in the hall here at six-thirty, and we can leave for our run as planned."

When John opened his door at six-thirty, he saw Bill and Fabio. Bill said, "Hope you don't mind, but I asked Fabio to join us. There will be police watching us along our route also."

John responded, "That sounds good to me. Why do we need people along the route? Do we anticipate any problems?"

Fabio responded, "Based on what happened when you arrived, we are not taking any chances. If there are problems, then we will be ready for them."

The three of them took the elevator to the lobby, dropped off their keys, and then walked out the front door. The sun was just coming up, and it was a beautiful day. There were already people running, walking, rollerblading, and riding bicycles.

When you leave the hotel, you have to go down about five steps to get to the street level. Then you have to walk about twenty feet to get to the street corner. You need to cross the street to get to the running path, which runs along the side of the beach. They all crossed over to the other side of the street, where there was a running path. At that time, John noticed four other people and said to Fabio, "In addition to the three of us, it looks like there will be four other people running."

"Yes, two of these guys will be in front of us, and two of them behind us, and they have guns under their sweat clothes."

Once on the other side of the street, Bill, Fabio, and John started their run. As they ran, John told them, "This run is one I used to do all the time when Kate and I were staying in the same hotel. This run will take us along the beach from Ipanema to the end of Copacabana beach."

Fabio mentioned, "As you can see, all along the way, there are police tracking us."

They all ran along the Ipanema beach. At about the one-and-a-half-mile point, in order to get to Copacabana beach, you need to go through a dark area away from the beach. There still is a path, but about a half-mile that is dark compared to running along the beach because it is shaded by buildings. They went through this dark area and got on the running path which goes along Copacabana beach.

When they were about a half-mile from the turn-around point, John pointed and said, "You see that large hill at the end of Copacabana beach? Along the side of the hill is a walkway that goes halfway around the hill over the water. Usually, there are people fishing along the side of the hill. There are about thirty feet from the water to the path. This gives you another beautiful view of Copacabana beach and the people in Rio. Sometimes they are surfing and swimming very close to the hill. Once we get there, we will walk along the walkway on the hill."

When they got to the end of Copacabana beach, they walked along the walkway by the side of the mountain and then back to the running path. At that point, John said, "You see that flea market is set up to sell clothing and paintings to the tourist. These flea markets are located in several spots in Ipanema and Copacabana.

The other item that you see along the running path is these little wood shacks with palm branch roofs. You can get any kind of drink at those shacks. In fact, if you want fresh cool coconut juice, they will open a coconut, while you wait and you can drink it out of a straw. Do you guys want to stop at these stands and get a drink once we reach the hotel?"

Fabio responded, "Sounds good to me."

So far, there was no encounter except for a few other people running or riding their bicycles. They started the run at about 6:30 a.m., so when they hit the turnaround point, they walked for about twenty minutes and then started running back on the pathway at about 7:15 a.m.

John was talking while he ran and said to Fabio and Bill, "You know you get to know people a lot better during a run. Also, as you run, you get to discuss and solve the problems of the world, at least you solve them in your mind."

They were approaching the dark area again, which was shaded by buildings and a small park. No one liked this area because it was a little dark. This park actually separated the road from the beach and had buildings on either side. If you want, you can cut through a park back to the beach or just keep on the running path, which will take you to the beach area.

When they left the Copacabana area and started into this darker area of the run, Fabio yelled out to the police, John, Bill, and Jeff, saying, "There appears to be a car heading toward us with four men in it. Let's increase our run speed so we can reach the park before the car reaches us."

The two police behind us and the ones in front drew their guns and raced ahead to stop the car before it reached us. Fabio got on his walkie-talkie and started to call in other support and also direct how to handle the car by yelling out, "Everyone converged on the car at the parking area. Bill and I will take John and Jeff into the park. The rest of you need to get the people in the car. I think I see machine guns."

They reached the park and made a quick left turn into the park when Fabio yelled, "Hit the ground behind that small stone wall."

There was a stone wall that shielded them from the street, and there were also some large rocks shielding them from the beach. Just at that moment, John caught out of the corner of his eye people leaning out of the car windows with guns. He yelled out, "They have guns. Keep your heads down."

They all hit the ground, and Bill and Fabio drew their guns. Before John put his head down, he saw several police cars converge on the car. There was a great deal of gunfire going on in the street. Just then, Fabio yelled out, "Turn around."

There were eight more people coming straight toward us from the beach. We were now being attacked from two sides. Fabio had a gun drawn and then pulled another small gun off his ankle and said, "John, take this gun. Use it when they come within range."

John replied, "Thanks Fabio."

This was a well-planned raid to kill John and the others. They had one group attacking from the beachside and the other group from the road. The buildings were stopping everyone from going in the other directions. So, John and everyone else were trapped in the park. Fabio got on his walkie-talkie and asked to have more people sent in to help. The police on the street were occupied with the people in the car and could not help John and others. Fabio then got a reply on his walkie-talkie, "Reinforcement will be there in two minutes."

John responded, "Fabio, this will be all over in thirty seconds." John then fired his gun at a guy that was rushing toward him and firing a machine gun.

He was very close, only about a few inches away and coming in from the side. John got him right in the heart and immediately hit the ground dead. As he hit the ground, the machine gun was thrown closer to where John was located. John was able to crawl to where the machine gun was located and got it. The people from the beach were still moving forward and firing their guns.

John then fired the machine gun at the people rushing toward him. It was clear they knew who John was since most of the gunfire was coming his way.

Fabio then fired a few shots and wounded one of the shooters. One of the shooters then threw a hand grenade close to where John was located. John could not grab it and send it back because it was between the shooters and him and probably a little closer to John. John told everyone to duck down and fired the machine gun just under the hand grenade, hoping it would fly back to where the shooters were located. He fired the machine gun, and it worked. The hand grenade flew back toward the gunman and exploded in the air, killing two more shooters.

Bill said, "John, I cannot believe what you did. That was nice."

Fabio responded, "Stay down. There are still four of them left with machine guns."

The other four gunmen kept coming forward, and firing their machine guns. John just took his machine gun and held it over the rock behind and held the trigger down, moving his arm back and forth, hoping that a bullet would hit one of the four shooters rushing toward them.

Just then, all the gunfire was slowing down and then stopped. Then John heard someone from behind them say to him, "Keep your heads down!" Then that same voice yelled to the shooter, "Give, up or you will die."

John stopped firing. There were ten police officers behind the wall with machine guns ready to fire at the gunman. The four shooters stopped immediately and dropped their weapons.

At that moment, there was no more gunfire from anyone. Fabio then said to John and Bill, "You guys stay here, and I will go investigate what happened in the street." The ten police officers also escorted the four shooters in the park to the street.

"After a few minutes, Fabio came back into the park and said, "Come on over to the police car. I want you to see if you recognize any of these people. It is safe." John and Fabio were standing outside the car, and Fabio pointed to the shooters and asked, "Have you ever seen these two people before?"

John looked at the two men and then said, "I do not know either of these people. How about you, Bill?"

"I do not know these two men. I have never seen them before. What about the other four guys?"

Fabio said, "The other four guys are not important people in the mob, but these two guys are top people in the mob and know what is going on. We are going to the police station, and you can follow in the police car behind us. The six bad guys on the street are dead. There are also two police officers that are dead."

John responded by saying, "Fabio, we better drop by the hotel, shower, and change, or no one will want to be close to us since we are filthy and stinking." Fabio turned to the police and said, "Separate the prisoners and begin questioning. I will be there as soon as we change." Two police cars took them back to the hotel. Fabio brought some clothes with him and changed in Bill's room.

John called Jeff to know what happened and said, "I don't think it would be productive for you to go to the police station with us. It would probably be best for you to focus on the database problem we discussed."

"I agree, John. Should I wait around for dinner with you and Bill?"

"Absolutely, we are going to go to a Brazilian restaurant tonight. I have been thinking about it for a while. Dinner is usually late here, so have a late lunch. I will call you as soon as we get back from the Police Station."

"Take care of yourself. No more gun stuff."

"I will also make sure they have a couple of extra security guards with you."

After they changed, John met Fabio in the lobby and said, "Make sure we have a couple of extra security guards on Jeff. He will probably stay in the hotel, but we should be careful."

"I have taken care of it. There will be two guards outside the hotel and two guards outside his door. I just talked with him about the security."

They all got in the police cars and headed to the police station. At the police station, Fabio said, "John, you and Bill can watch everything from this window. You will be able to see them, but they cannot see you. We will be questioning them in each of these rooms."

John responded, "Do you have a phone I can use?"

Fabio pointed at the phone in the room and said to dial nine for an outside line, and you will be able to call the US. John got Jim on the phone, so he could give him an update on what happened this morning.

John summarized everything by saying, "During my run, about twelve people tried to get us, but we stopped them. There were six of them killed and two police officers. We are questioning two of the leaders now and will give you a call later today and give you an update. Please let Kate know I am OK.

Can you also call Jeff and Bill's wives to let them know that they are OK since this may make the news?"

The questioning went on for about eight hours with a few breaks. Bill and John were watching everything through the one-way glass so they could see and hear everything, but the people on the other side could not see them. Fabio knocked on their door, and John said, "Come in."

Fabio came into the room and said, "You heard most of what they said. It was determined that they were taking orders from one of the mob leaders in Rio, which the police had been trying to catch.

They gave us the names of two of the mob leaders, but they were not sure which mob leader it was since they saw both at meetings. One thing is for sure. The mob leader was taking direction from someone in the United States. They were told to put together their people and then attack us at the airport, and when that did not work, they were told that John would probably be running that morning and they should try to kill John and the others with John at that time. The mob was given a lot of money to kill John."

After John got that information, John made a call back to Jim and briefed him by saying, "Jim, the problem is really back at that end. The mob bosses are taking direction from someone in the states. We suspected this before, but now we have confirmed it through these two people that were captured.

I will head back on the first flight I can catch, which will be Sunday night. We need to increase the speed of our investigation on the US end. Until we get the person in the US that is paying everyone off in all these countries, then no one is safe. We better put an extra security guard on Kate until we catch this person."

Jim responded, "We will step up security. You do the same on that end. Kate has been focusing on that short list back at this end. Let me get her now. Please stay on the phone."

Jim was able to find her, and he briefed her on what John had told him as she came on the speaker phone, "John, I heard what happened to you during your run. Please be very careful. Now to answer your question; We have the list down to a few people, and when you return, I think we can get the list narrowed down to one company and person."

Fabio called out to John, "The US Ambassador is on the other line, and he would like to talk with you."

John said to Kate, "Did you hear that, Kate?"

"Yes, the US Ambassador to Brazil wants to talk with you. It seems like you are an important guy over there. Don't let it go to our head."

"It won't. There seems to be some people here that really like me and some that hate me. You take care. I love you, Kate."

"I love you, John. Be careful."

John hung up with Kate and then flipped it to the other line and said, "Hello, Mr. Ambassador, how are you feeling?"

"I am fine, John. Thank you for asking. How is Jeff doing?"

"We left him at the hotel today so he could get some rest. He is doing fine. How can I help you?"

"John, I heard about what happened to you today. How are you doing? I am sorry that this is happening to you. You know I have been here three years and never had any problems."

"I understand that this is not entirely a Brazil problem. We are checking into some people in the US that may be making all this happen."

"John, can you, Bill, and Jeff join me for dinner tonight? I think it would be good for you to taste some real Brazilian food at a Brazilian Barbeque restaurant in Ipanema called Porchi. Do not worry. I will have sufficient security and we can talk about the next steps we should take in Brazil. The Chief of Police in Rio will be joining us along with Juan Carlos."

"That would be great. I promised the guys a nice Brazilian dinner. You must have read my mind."

"I will pick you up at your hotel at eight."

After this call, John got back to Fabio and said, "Fabio, I started out with a run this morning, and it looks like I have been here all day. Are we all done? If we are, can you take Bill and me back to the hotel?"

Fabio responded, "Thanks for hanging in with us through all this. We are done, and we have a car with two police cars to escort you back to the hotel."

John and Bill got back to the hotel at about 7:30 p.m. and went up to Jeff's room. John knocked on the door, and when Jeff opened it up, he said, "Jeff, we have all been invited to dinner with the US Ambassador. We are all going to have a Brazilian barbeque at the Porchi close to the hotel, which is one of the best restaurants in Rio. It has a great salad bar and waiters that just keep coming out with different meats on a skewer. They cut the meat at the table, and they keep bringing the meat out. As long as you keep the button, they give you a green side up. When you turn it over to the red side, they stop bringing the meat to you.

After that meal, you do not want to eat meat for a month. The other item that we need to have when we go is caipirinha which is a drink many people in Brazil drink. If you drink about four caipirinhas, you do not feel any pain. So be careful.

The ambassador said he would pick us up at the hotel around eight. Dinner in Brazil starts later than in the US. Actually, eight is early for dinner. Don't be surprised to see children at dinner after eleven. Dinner for many people in Brazil starts at nine."

Jeff responded, "I'm ready. Let's go."

"OK, let's meet in the hall outside our doors, and we can go downstairs at about 7:50 p.m."

They all met as planned, and the guards by their rooms followed them down to the lobby. One of them stayed guard at the rooms to make sure no one went into their rooms while they were not there. When they stepped outside the hotel, they could look across the street and see the running path along the beach, and there were still people walking and running along the path.

It was a beautiful night with the moon lit up the ocean. In fact, it was so bright you could see a couple of wooded islands off in the distance. John mentioned to Bill and Jeff, "If you wake up anytime between midnight and six in the morning and look at the beach, then you will see about fifty to a hundred people just sitting on the sand on a blanket looking at the ocean."

Just then, the Ambassador's car pulled up in front of the hotel with two police cars. One of them was in front, and the other followed the car. Jeff and Bill got in the car, and they all headed off to the restaurant. As they approached the restaurant, they noticed several police in front of the restaurant and also inside.

The Chief of Police, Juan Carlos, and Fabio were at a round table inside the restaurant and waved to the US Ambassador, Jeff, Bill, and John as they came in the front door. The round table was in the back of the restaurant, and there were police at the front of the restaurant and next to the round table. There were also police outside the restaurant. It was a safe environment.

At dinner, Juan Carlos commented, "John, the day you were announced as starting the medical project again, I got a call from the mob warning me that my staff and I better watch our backs because our lives will be in danger if the project is continued.

We wanted to try to capture some of the mob leaders then, but they were difficult to find. Also, when you finally find them, it is difficult to convict them because it is difficult to find people that will testify against the mob. The mob goes after people's families. If someone talks against them, I believe the day you said you were coming, we got another call from the mob."

John responded, "As I mentioned to you when we talked, I believe you and the people working on the Medical Project would have been killed whether the US was announced as starting the project again or not. There is someone who will lose a great deal of money if this project continues because they are collecting money from the way the current medical process is run.

The US Ambassador asked, "John, what person do you think would lose the most money if this project is successful?"

There are a few people and companies that would lose money. We are looking at each one of them. Things are structured differently around the world, although some large medical groups and people are involved with medicine no matter where it is in the world. As new and different approaches are found to cure diseases, they will either have to adjust or lose money.

One example is that we will be able to find diseases faster than we ever did before because you will be able to detect why they occur sooner from information that is being entered into that database. Therefore, there are people that will lose money.

The flow of money in the medical industry will change since you are spending more money on finding things quicker rather than trying to cure them after they have gone through your whole body. This reduces the medicines that have to be used when diseases are let go. Also, this will reduce the high cost of hospitals and medical insurance. So, people that own hospitals or distribute those medicines that help people after they get the disease could lose some money.

Therefore, there are people that do not want to change where money is flowing today, and those are the people that may want to stop this project.

The US Ambassador's eyes were wide open, and you could tell he was excited when he said, "I never thought the Medical Project was that big. We will be able to detect where diseases are coming from before they spread all over the world. That alone is excellent.

John, do you and your friends think you will have more time to go into this in more detail tomorrow? My wife has plans to be with her friends in the afternoon so I may be free. I can pick you guys up around 1 p.m. and take you to a place where we can watch people jump off a mountain in a parachute. While we watch these parachute jumps, we will be able to talk."

John responded, "That sounds good to me as long as we are only watching parachute jumps. I definitely do not want to participate. How about you guys?

Bill, Jeff, Juan Carlos, and Fabio said, "OK!"

Bill then said, "Will Fabio and you, Mr. Ambassador, handle all the security?"

Fabio responded, "OK!"

The Chief of Police changed the subject and then said, "John, how do we know that the US will stay on the Medical Project and not leave as they did before?"

"My wife and I would not have come back to work on the project if we were not promised by the President of the United States and our Government that once we restart the Medical Project, it would not be canceled."

Juan Carlos then said, "I would like to help you find the person in the US who is responsible for all these killings around the world. Once we find him, then we can get the proof we need to get the people back here."

The Police Chief said, "I thought we had enough proof to convict the mob leaders."

Fabio responded, "Right now, we have it down to two mob leaders."

The Police Chief then said, "OK, if Juan Carlos goes, then I would also like to send Fabio. Until we catch the person who is responsible, I want to make sure we supply protection for Juan Carlos."

John told them, "I think that is a great idea. I will expect you as soon as you can get away from what you are doing now."

All had a great dinner and a lot of caipirinhas which is a very sweet and strong alcoholic drink. On the way back to the hotel, John mentioned to Jeff and Bill, "How about sleeping late and running at about ten tomorrow morning? We then can meet at about noon outside our doors on our floor and go to the lobby to meet with the Ambassador at one as he requested.

They all got back to their rooms and had no trouble sleeping that night.

Lunch with the Ambassador

John woke up at seven-thirty in the morning and decided to have breakfast at eight and then exercise at ten. When he woke up, he told the guards outside his door his plan for this morning, and they said they would be prepared.

When John left his room at eight, Bill was waiting for him. Bill said, "Is it OK if I have breakfast and exercise with you?"

"Sure, you can join me. I was going to get one of the other guards to watch me this morning and let you sleep late today."

"I'm up and ready to go."

"OK, let's catch the elevator to the breakfast room."

Two guards accompanied them to the breakfast room, and one stayed downstairs to guard Jeff. When they were seated in the restaurant, Bill mentioned to John, "They have some of the best coffee in the world. It is hard to drink any other coffee after you have had this. Even the decaf coffee is great."

"I agree! Just don't have regular coffee before you go to bed, or you will be up all night." Then he looked off into the distance and said, "I still cannot get over this view."

"You are right. This restaurant has to have one of the best views in the world, and it also has some of the best breakfast buffets in the world."

After forty minutes, Bill and John were done with breakfast, and John said, "OK, I am going to head off to my room and give Kate a call, and then we can meet for a run on the treadmill at ten."

Bill responded, "I think I will call my wife also. See you at ten."

When John got into his room, he picked up the phone and called Kate. Kate was just waking up and said, "Hello."

John responded, "Hi Kate, this is John. Hope I did not wake you up but wanted to try to reach you before the day began."

"It is nice to hear from you. How come you did not call last night?"

"I had Brazilian barbeque with the US Ambassador, Juan Carlos, and a few others and got in a little late, so I didn't want to wake you up."

"How come the US Ambassador is hanging out with you guys?"

"He is interested in the project. I believe he used to be a doctor before they made him Ambassador. Plus, since this project is worldwide, he is interested in the effects in Brazil. In fact, he wants to know more about the project today. We will be going out at about one to watch some parachute jumps."

"John, make sure you only watch and not do any parachute jumping."

"Don't worry. I hate heights. How is Katelin doing?"

"She is doing great. In fact, we are going to lunch today."

"Well, you two ladies have fun. I love you both."

"I love you. Be careful over there."

After the call, John walked over to the window. His room had a bedroom area and also a sitting area. The TV could be swung around so you could watch it from the sitting area or the bedroom. John and Kate always were given this type of room whenever they stayed there because they had lived there for five months and the hotel always upgraded them.

The view was of the beach, running path, and street. It was a spectacular view of the ocean. You could just look out the window and dream. John used to get some of his best ideas and said a few prayers while looking out that window.

Right now, he was praying so that Katelin's cancer would never come back. In addition, he also thinks about how to restart the Medical Project and who could be trying to stop the Program.

John then looked at his watch and said to himself, boy, how time flies when you are having fun. I better get ready for this run on the treadmill.

In a few minutes, John was ready for his run. He exited the door, and Bill was waiting and said, "Well, are you ready for this?"

John responded, "Well if we are going to continue to eat like this, we need to do this."

After the run, John told Bill, "I am just going to do some work in my room until about 12:50 p.m. I will see you outside our doors at that time."

"OK, John, see you at 12:50 p.m."

John left his room at 12:50 p.m., and Bill and Jeff were waiting in the hall. Two of the guards followed them down the elevator, and the other stayed behind to guard the rooms. When they reached the lobby, Juan Carlos and Fabio were there waiting. Everyone said hello and then went to the front door.

When they went out the door, John looked at the beach and said, "Hey guys, this is beautiful, isn't it?"

Juan Carlos responded, "You really picked an excellent hotel."

Just then, the US Ambassador's car pulled up with two police cars. One of the police cars was in front, and one was in the back. The Ambassador opened up his window and said, "Come on in. I believe all six of us can fit in this car."

"We all got in, and I noticed we all seemed to be dressed in our shorts, shirt, and sneakers. The car began pulling away from the hotel when the Ambassador told us, "This place is just about ten miles north of the hotel. There is a small restaurant just off the beach. We can watch the parachuters land on the beach. I made some reservations for us at that restaurant."

John asked the Ambassador, "How do these parachuters start their jumps?"

"They start their jumps from a mountain and then drift on down to the beach."

Just then, the car was pulling off the highway and onto a road leading to the beach restaurant. The ambassador opened up the sunroof and pointed upward, saying, "See that mountain over there. There is a flat top on the mountain, and people run off the mountain. There is a person now taking off from the mountain. They all use these air foil-type parachutes. You can see about ten in the sky right now."

Just then, the car pulled up to the restaurant, and everyone got out of the car and looked up and got a better view of the people in the air. There were a couple of tables close to the beach. The people were actually landing on a strip of beach that was flat and about one hundred feet long. The restaurant and table were on a concrete slab about 15 feet above the place where the people were landing on the beach. One table was for the Ambassador, and the other was for security. The police were located at other points around the restaurant in case there was a problem.

The Ambassador looked John directly in the eye and was very serious when he said, "John, how do you plan on getting the world to agree on using this Medical Project? Also, what are your plans to restart the program?"

John looked at the Ambassador and said, "Mr. Ambassador, I will answer your questions if you can let me know why you are so interested in the Medical Project."

"I believe you know I am a doctor in the US. I practice internal medicine in Virginia. I got out of medicine because I could not make money as a doctor with the new rules. I was really practicing medicine almost as a hobby. So I am very interested in the Medical Industry.

I became the Ambassador because I was getting a little frustrated with medicine. I spent more time filling out forms and justifying what I was doing rather than actually practicing medicine. So when the President asked me to be the US Ambassador to Brazil, I took the job. I guess you can say I am on leave from medicine."

John then responded, "That is a sad story. To answer your question about how we plan on getting the world to agree to use this Medical Project.

Well, the Medical Project began about three years ago when the President went first to congress and then the senate to get their approval. They did get approval. We also got an agreement that what we and the twenty other countries that were working with us in the program came up with would be used throughout the US. So, they funded the first phase of the project, and we proceeded.

In addition, our government did get the other twenty country governments to agree to the same thing that our congress and senate agreed. Once we got the agreements, we asked the Presidents of those countries to give us their best person to lead this for their country. We had all these agreements, and people committed about two and a half years ago.

We completed the first phase of the project, and when the US went for funding for the second phase of the project, we were turned down. So the US killed the project for the US, but it proceeded in many other countries.

When the project was killed in the US, I found out that my daughter got cancer, so my wife and I went on a leave of absence. They asked me to return about one week ago. I did if they would guarantee that the project would be funded until it is completed. My daughter was in remission, so my wife and I decided to come back on the project. Since there was a recommitment by our government and the UN to complete the project and use the results."

The Ambassador looked at John with concern and said, "How is your daughter doing? We are getting close on cures for different types of cancer."

"Thanks for asking, Mr. Ambassador. Right now, she is feeling great and ready to go back to work and wanted us to take this project."

The Ambassador put his thumb up and said, "That is great. I have another question. How did you get your wife to work with you on the same project?"

"We had been working in the same agency, and sometimes when projects are big, we get on the same project. Now let me answer your second question about how we plan to restart the program. First, we need to find the person that is trying to stop the Medical Project and bring that person to justice.

Then I believe we can add all the countries to the project. The computers now can handle the load, and with the internet, it now can be done. So we will get the President to address the United Nations again and get all countries to put their best people on the project.

The more countries that we add, the more information we can gather and the more reliable the output to the doctors and people. They will join because it will reduce the cost of medical expenses in their countries and also deaths,

We had to screen out some countries initially so we could get the program going, but now we should be able to open it up to everyone, and everyone, I am sure, will join."

The Ambassador raised his finger again and asked another question, "How do you expect to get agreement from all the nations on using the Medical Project after it is done?"

"The details and architecture are done, and I have found that once you get good technical people that their president has appointed on the project and agreement by the countries, they will use what we come up with within their country."

For the rest of the day, they just had their lunch, drank a few beers, and watched the people coming out of the sky. It was a memorable day. At about six, they all got into the car and headed back to the hotel.

John asked Jeff and Bill, "What about having Feijoada (Fish-Wada is how it sounds in English) at the hotel tomorrow?"

Bill said, "That sounds good to me."

Jeff asked, "What is Feijoada?"

John responded, "Feijoada is a traditional meal in Brazil. It was originally served as leftovers in low-income families in Brazil. In other words, you could have pig ears or feet boiling in a soup. In the hotel and other places, it is not leftovers but delicious dishes, and it just so happens that the hotel we are staying at has the best Feijoada in Brazil."

Jeff responded, "It is just what everyone needs at this point, another buffet."

John responded, "The only reason I run is so that he can eat all this good food. Two buffets in two days would mean a few extra sit-ups and a few extra miles."

Jeff responded, and Bill agreed, "OK, let's have Feijoada but no dinner tonight for me. What time are you waking up to run?"

John responded and said, "No dinner for me either. It is the treadmill for me. I have had enough excitement on this trip. Let's run at about nine in the morning and then maybe go for the Feijoada at about eleven. I think they start serving it at the hotel at eleven, and it ends at four."

Bill said, "Sounds like a plan. Mr. Ambassador, can you join us tomorrow?"

The Ambassador said, "First, let me say, I really enjoyed the day with you guys. It was fun. Let me check with my wife and see what she has planned."

John responded, "OK, Mr. Ambassador, thanks for the great day. This type of day is something you never forget. Hope to see you tomorrow."

After returning to the hotel, John, Jeff, and Bill went to the rooms and went straight to bed.

———◆———

FEIJOADA AND THE HIPPY FAIR

As planned, Bill and John woke up, did the treadmill, and then John called Jeff at about ten-thirty in the morning and said, "Are you ready for Feijoada?"(in English it is pronounced fishwada)

"Yes, I will meet you outside our doors at 11 a.m."

Jeff, Bill, and John all met outside their rooms and had a short discussion on where to go for the Feijoada at the hotel. Bill said, "I made a reservation for us at the restaurant on the second floor. I was told that on Sunday, people come from all over Rio for this Feijoada."

John had a smile on his face when he said, "This should be fun. I tell my wife when I go on these trips, I always cheat on her and eat all the food I am not supposed to eat. OK, guys, this is why we exercise. Let's go eat this great food."

They all got in the elevator with two guards and went to the second floor. John thought of Kate when he got off the elevator and said to Bill and Jeff, "This brings some memories of when Kate and I were staying at the hotel, and they wanted us to take a tour of all of this food. It was great but what we found is that if you are a vegetarian like Kate, then this is probably not the right place to eat since almost everything has some type of a meat base. So Kate and I went to another restaurant to eat."

Jeff responded, "Well, if we had a problem with meat, then the Brazilian Barbeque would have done us in."

John smiled and pointed to each of the separate rooms full of food and said, "I think this room is for drinks and appetizers, and that room is for desserts, and the big room is where we sit and have the main course. They don't come to you with the food, but you go get what you want."

The table they had reserved had an ocean view. The guards were at the table between them and the door, so they could stop any people that would come toward their table.

It was a little early for caipirinha, but Bill, Jeff, and John got one anyway and just sat at the table and looked at the beautiful view. The people were walking and running along the beach. On Sundays, they close off the street, and there are people singing, playing instruments, and selling clothing, souvenirs, and food all along the closed-off area. Also, there are people running, walking, skating, and playing different games on the beach.

In Rio de Janeiro, Monday thru Friday, they have the traffic goes one way into the city from 7 a.m. until 10 a.m. Then, from 4 p.m. until 7 p.m., the traffic goes one way out of the city. On Saturday and Sunday, the traffic is closed off from 8 a.m. until 8 p.m. along the six miles of beach, so the street is open for people walking and running.

The people in Brazil know how to relax and have a good time, and Sundays in Rio is that time for many people. So Jeff, Bill, and John just looked out the window in the restaurant and watched all this activity going on while they slowly ate their food.

When they were almost done eating, John got Jeff and Bill's attention and said, "Look, Juan Carlos, Fabio, and the US Ambassador and his wife, Joan, are here." They all came over to their table, and John, Jeff, and Bill all stood up. Everyone began shaking hands and hugging.

When the US Ambassador's wife came over to John, she had a tear in her eye and gave John a hug, and said, "I want to thank you again for saving my husband's life."

John responded with a smile and said, "He is a great man."

Joan then went on, "We were going to the Hippie Fair and wanted to know if all of you wanted to join us? It is just a few blocks from our hotel, and we have sufficient security so we could have a good time, and you will not have to worry about security."

John responded by telling Bill and Jeff, "The Hippie Fair is a place where they sell art, clothing, and many other things local to Brazil. Kate and I used to go to the Hippie Fair every Sunday when we lived in Rio. On the way back, we always stopped at McDonald's and got a milkshake and fries. It is worth seeing. I recommend we go."

Bill responded, and Jeff also was affirmative, "You are batting 100%, John. Your recommendations have been great. I say let's go. It sounds like a good place to be on a Sunday. I need to get a gift for my wife. I guess we need to get back at around five so we can get to the airport and catch our flight."

John looked at the Ambassador's wife and, with a smile, said, "Well, it looks like we are going to join you, and thanks for thinking of us. I think we all have to get a gift for our wives."

The walk to the Hippie Fair was like all walks in Ipanema and walked along the beach. This time they could walk on the street that was closed off for about two blocks and then inland about two blocks to a square in the city where the vendors set up booths and sell their goods.

John said when they arrived, "I really like the music at this fair. There is a person that plays popular songs on a guitar and sells them on CDs. I need to find something for my wife. I think I will look for some art. She likes paintings with sunflowers.

The US Ambassador said, "Do you want Joan and me to give you a hand?"

"Yes, let's stick together."

All of a sudden, John did see a painting that he knew Kate would like. It was a painting that showed a field of sunflowers. When he saw the painting, he told the Ambassador and his wife, "That is it. I have never seen a painting like that before. I know Katelin would love it."

Joan said, "You know you are expected to negotiate a price."

John responded, "I really don't like to negotiate, but since there was no price on the painting, I will do it. This also gives me a chance to practice my Portuguese."

John was able to negotiate a price with the vendor, so he got the painting. John knew his wife wanted her own frame, so John was able to negotiate for just the painting without the frame. The vendor then took it out of the frame, rolled it up, and put it in a hard cylinder. John paid the vendor and thanked him for the great painting.

John kept looking around and then saw Juan Carlos and Fabio. He walked up to them and asked, "Did you find anything you liked."

Juan Carlos responded, "Not yet, but we are still looking. How about you?"

John held up his cylinder and said, "I found a painting that I believe Kate will like. Hey, when are you guys coming to the US? There is good shopping in the US, and we can use you on the project."

Juan Carlos responded, "I need a couple of days to finalize the work I am doing here. We are trying to identify the Brazilian mob bosses that could be involved in trying to stop the Medical Project. My guess is we can join you sometime this week."

John responded, "That sounds good to me."

They were done with the Hippy Fair around five and headed back to the hotel. They all decided to skip dinner before the flight since everyone was still full from the Feijoada and the airlines usually give you a dinner on the flight.

They all decided to sign on to their computers, answer some emails and then start packing. They needed to leave for the airport around 7 p.m., so they did not have too much time.

John was also able to call Kate before leaving and asked, "How are you and Katelin doing? Does she have any pain?"

Kate responded, "I am doing OK, and Katelin seems to be doing OK. We both have two bodyguards from the agency. One watches things going on inside, and the other watches things going on outside, so we feel very safe. You have a safe trip home."

"I love you, Kate. Tell Katelin I love her and will see you both soon."

The ride back to the airport was uneventful, which is what everyone wanted. The overnight flight back was also uneventful, which is what you want. They arrived in Miami at about six-thirty in the morning and then got their connection to Washington. They arrived in Washington about eleven in the morning, and when John got home, Kate was home. Kate had taken half a day off, and John was going to do the same thing.

Kate put her arms around John when he came in the door and said, "It is great to have you home."

"It's great to be home. I missed you."

"I bought you a gift from Rio."

"Where is it? You know I love gifts."

"Here it is."

Kate took the cylinder and then took out the painting. John then glanced at Kate, her eyes twinkling with joy—evident that what he had done was a good thing.

John said, "I know you like sunflowers. There are more sunflowers in the painting than I have ever seen anywhere."

"I love it. I love you. You must be tired. Do you want to sleep for a while, and then we can go for dinner?"

"I think I will go for a run, and then we can go for dinner. How is our Katelin doing?"

"I worry about her every day. She still has a little pain, but the doctor says there is no cancer. You know the cancer she had was killed at the original source, but like all cancer, it is not the original location that will kill you but where it travels to from that point. All that is needed is one cell to travel someplace else in your body, and it starts growing."

"I know. Did you ask her to stay with us tonight?

"I did, but she is focused on work and said she wants to stay at her apartment."

That night after Kate fell asleep, John went to his computer, and again as he usually does, he started looking on the internet for information on cancer cures. He also gave Katelin a call and talked with her briefly.

John spent a great deal of time gathering information on the internet concerning answers to questions he had about Katelin's cancer. He knew the ideal system to use in this situation would be the medical system he was developing for the project, but it was not ready to be used, so he was just searching for new treatments using the internet. Any spare moment he or Kate had was used by either talking with Katelin or finding possible cures for her cancer. Even though Katelin was in remission, John never stopped looking just in case it would come back.

DINNER WITH KATELIN

The alarm rang at six in the morning. John and Kate both woke up and went out for their run. The security guards followed behind them in their car. After their run and a quick breakfast, they both were ready to get in the car and head off to work. One guard stayed at the house, and two guards with the car driver picked them up, and they were on the way to work. Once they arrived at the office, John reviewed with the team what had happened in Rio.

He then asked Kate, "Can I look at the list of people that you and the team came up with that could be causing all the deaths?"

Kate responded, "Here is a list of the entire medical lobbyists. Here is the same list, only it is in order of the amount of money being spent. We are going to find out from this list who has been making calls to Rio de Janeiro."

John also asked, "Did you ask our legal team to get involved to ensure that we are not breaking any laws by getting a list of who was making calls to Rio de Janeiro?"

Paul, who was working with Kate, responded, "We are ok. We have been cleared."

John looked at Paul, smiled, and said, "It is so great to have you on this project with us."

Jim's secretary popped her head into the conference room and asked, "Kate can you and John meet with Jim? He would like to talk with you now if it fits in with your schedule."

John and Kate went to Jim's office, briefed him on what they were doing, and then asked, "OK, we briefed you on what we were up to. What did you want to see us about?"

Jim responded, "We were lucky that we contacted Rio de Janeiro and were able to divert what they had planned. When they saw that they could not kill the medical project in Brazil, they went after Buenos Aires.

He told us that some people in Buenos Aires were killed. They are still going to continue working on the medical project even if people were killed. It will be at a slower pace. They also asked when we thought we would find the person responsible for all the killings?"

John responded, "I think we are getting close. At least now we know it is someone in the U.S., and they have made calls to Rio."

Jim changed the subject, saying, "At this point, I don't think it is necessary to go to Hong Kong. We had sufficient proof the problem was here in the U.S. What do you think, John?"

"You are right. Our next trip will be to the location of the person we suspect is making the killings."

Jim then mentioned, "OK, I am going to brief the President. He said to keep him updated weekly."

Kate and John then continued to work with the team in coming up with the list of people. They all left the agency at around 7 p.m. that night. John and Kate went home to Katelin. Outside there were a couple of security guards and a car to take them to where they needed to go.

Kate told John, "I called Katelin, and she said she would have dinner with us tonight.

"Great! Should we pick her up at work?

"Yes, I told her we would pick her up at work and then take her back to get her car after dinner."

The car arrived at Katelin's work, and Katelin popped out of the door as soon as the car pulled up, saying, "I almost forgot that you guys now have a car and bodyguards."

John asked, "Katelin, how are you feeling? I really missed you."

"I think I am doing better than you. At least no one is shooting at me. How are things going at work? Are you getting any closer to finding the person responsible for all these problems?"

"I think we are closer to finding the person who is causing all these problems; therefore, things are going well at work."

The car arrived at the restaurant, and they all went in. The security guards sat at one table, and Kate, Katelin, and John sat at another. When they were seated, Katelin asked, "Daddy, why do you want to do this project?

John responded, "I really think this project will make a difference in the world we live in today. I like to work on things that can make things better for everyone and where we can make a difference. Of course, I am also interested in money, and usually, when you are working on something important, then you usually get paid appropriately. The main thing is that we are working on something that will make the world a better place. I only hope this comes out the way your mom and I want it to."

"But Daddy, you are risking your life."

"With the security we now have, I believe we will be safe. The person that needs to worry is the person responsible for doing all these evil things.

After they all finished their meals, the car dropped Katelin off at her car. There were two security guards that followed Katelin to her apartment, and a car with two security guards followed Kate and John back to their house.

People Trying to Stop Project

The next day seemed like Groundhog Day, which like the movie, had the same thing happening as the past days. The alarm went off. They went for a run and then went off to work.

When they arrived at work, it looked like Paul and some of the team had been pulling an all-nighter. Paul said, "We narrowed the list of people that could be responsible for the killing down to ten. From the ten, there were five that would lose money if the Medical Project was successful."

John and Kate knew all five of these people. They looked at the list for a while, and Kate said, "I believe we can get this list down to two people. The other three are people that have supported us in this project in every way. I am convinced that the two people that could be responsible for the killings are one of these two guys. One is located in Dallas and the other in New York City."

John responded, "Excellent! How about calls to Rio de Janeiro? Which has made calls to Rio?"

Paul responded back, "Both of the offices for these people made calls to Rio de Janeiro, but the office in Dallas made more calls."

Kate then said, "The other item I am concerned about is who was leaking information to these people from the agency. That person could have helped this person kill the project and also could have helped this person attempt to have John and others killed in Rio."

John then said, "Let's focus on the person responsible for all the killings. If we get that person, we will find the leak. It looks to me like this person in Dallas made more calls to Rio and also has a little bit more to lose than the person in New York.

Let's make an appointment for me to see him tomorrow. I know him. His name is Sam Jacob. He is the President of a company called Medical Resource International. They do work all over the world. This is a company that controls several billion dollars in the medical area and is responsible for the way most things are run today in the US and around the world. Companies like this one were concerned about any change that could affect incoming money?"

Jeff mentioned, "Should we see if Fabio and Juan Carlos can meet you in Dallas before the meeting."

Kate responded, "Excellent idea Jeff. I believe there is a direct flight from Rio de Janeiro to Dallas, so they could get in around 7 a.m. and meet John there at the agency at about 11 a.m. Let's set up the meeting with Sam at 3 p.m. John, who else do you want to take with you?"

"I think I will just need a security person with me. See if we can get Bill. He brings me luck."

That night Jim and his wife wanted to have dinner with John and Kate. Doris made all the arrangements and also came along. They were all going to meet at the restaurant.

Doris arrived first and greeted John and Kate. She first gave Kate a hug and then looked at John with a smile and said, "It's good to have you back. Kate and I have been working together on Medical Project when you were gone. Jim is sharing me with you until I can bring his new assistant up to speed. Kate and I have become good friends. In fact, we have lunch tomorrow, right, Kate?

Kate smiled at Doris and said, "Yes, I am looking forward to our lunch."

"Thank you, Kate. I really appreciate the time you are spending with me to get me up to speed. I can't wait until I can be on the project full-time."

Doris turned to John with a serious look on her face and said, "Kate and I are both concerned about all the attempts on your life. Do you think you will need more security?"

"Jim has put enough security on me. I should be OK."

Jim and his wife Diane arrived at that moment, and Diane gave Kate and John a kiss on the cheek and said, "I want you guys to be very careful. You are the best friends we have, and the country needs you."

Diane and Jim have been married for thirty years, and they have known Kate and John for twenty-five years. Diane is an African American and about the same size and shape as Kate.

At dinner, there was a lot of conversation about the project and also the future. It was a dinner that friends have and intend to have many more times. After dinner, everyone went home.

JOHN TRAVELS TO DALLAS FOR A MEETING

John woke up at about six and turned to Kate, saying, "I love you. Do you want to go for a run?"

"I love you too, but I am not going for a run. I will makc you some coffee, and we can have it when you return. See you after your run."

"OK, see you at around 7:30 a.m."

When John got back from his run, he showered and got dressed. He then went into the living room, and Kate was there, and he said, "Well, I am glad that is over. It is great just to sit here with you and have some coffee and orange juice. Did you use the new squeezer we got? I like it. Nothing like squeezing oranges the old fashion way."

"So when you see Sam Jacob, what are you going to say?"

"Why are you killing all of these people? No, not really. I need to ask him a few questions, and if he talks to me straight, then I will know he is not the person. If he lies, then we got him."

"If he is the guy, then you know he will not admit it, and we will have to prove it. I think we will need to be prepared and get a search warrant quickly if we find Sam is responsible for these killings. This will then allow us to get more proof and also find other names in Brazil and other countries that are associated with these killings."

"OK, Kate, my love. I better get going to the airport, and you need to get to work. You be careful."

Kate was working in her office, and Doris stopped by and stuck her head in her door, and said, "Kate, it is time for lunch. Do you want to go to a spot I consider one of the best in Washington for lunch?"

Kate responded, "Yes, let's go!"

They then got in Doris's car and went to the restaurant. At lunch, Kate said to Doris, "OK, let's not talk about work. Let's talk about you. Do you have a boyfriend?"

"I have been going out with a person for about a year, and he is rich, handsome, and seems to be as interested in me as I am in him. In fact, we have eaten lunch here a couple of times. He lives in Texas but spends a great deal of time in Washington. In fact, we have plans to meet at a beach house in Annapolis tonight. We have gone there a couple of times. I really look forward to seeing him."

"Do you think it is getting close to a wedding proposal?"

"I think it is, but we have not discussed it."

Kate had a big smile on her face and grabbed Doris's hand and said, "Do you want to bring him over for dinner sometime?"

With some disappointment on Doris's face, she said, "He is a hard guy to schedule time with, but I will try."

Kate said with a look of urgency, "I want to meet this guy. Just pick a date, and I will make sure that John and I are there."

Based on the short meeting Kate had with Doris, you could tell they were going to be good friends. Lunch went quickly because both of them had meetings back at the office, and after about an hour, they headed back to work.

John arrived in Dallas and went directly to the government agency. He was greeted by people there that he would be working with and also saw that Fabio and Juan Carlo had arrived as planned. He was delighted to see them both, and they all hugged, which is usually done among friends in Latin America.

John then said with a very serious look on his face, "It is great to see you guys again. We think the guy we will be seeing today could be the one responsible for all of the killings, but we are not sure yet. The purpose of this meeting will be to determine if he is the guy."

"Juan Carlos said, "How do you want to ensure that this is the right guy? What do you need us to do?

In this meeting, there may not be anything you need to do, but if we get an indication, he is the guy, then I may need you to when we perform a search in his company and home to see if you are able to recognize the names of mob bosses better than I. We will know if he is the guy if he is not open to our questions or lies. I will do the talking since I know Sam Jacob."

Juan Carlos responded, "OK, we are ready."

They took a car with two cars of agency security people. When they arrived, they all went to the front desk, and John said, "Hello, we are here to see Sam Jacob. My name is John Colombo."

"Yes, we are expecting you. I believe you are early. The meeting is in the board room. Follow this lady, and she will take you to the room."

There was a special elevator that they had to take in order to get to the board room. The board room was huge with a U-shaped wooden table with all kinds of audio and visual equipment.

When they arrived, Sam's secretary was there to meet them and said, "Sam and his team were running a little late, and you are a little early. Please wait in the board room."

John responded, "OK!"

The only people in the room were people from John's team. John told his team, "You guys wait here. I am going to look into that office over there." So John wandered off to the little room in the far corner of the conference room. He mentioned to the team, "This looks like Sam's office. You guys let me know if someone is coming. I want to look around his office."

He looked across his desk. He noticed that Jim's administrative assistant, Doris's name, and telephone number were written on a pad. He also noticed several numbers from Brazil. Just then, Juan Carlos called out with an urgent tone, "Some people are coming."

John then quickly went back into the boardroom. Just as he entered the boardroom, the door opened, and Sam and five of his people came in.

They all sat down, and Sam asked John, "Hi John, nice to see you again. What is this all about?"

John looked Sam directly in the eye, and with a tone that indicated that he was upset, said, "Sam, you are aware of the Medical Project, correct?"

Sam acknowledged that he did, so John continued.

"I was working on the project when it was stopped in the U.S. In some of the other countries where the project was not stopped, there are people being killed? Do you know why these people are being killed? Do you have any idea who could be killing these people?"

Sam answered this question with an attitude indicating that he did not care that people were being killed, "My guess is that people are being killed because people like the Medical Project they have today and do not want it changed. I think things are fine the way medicine is being handled today. I have no idea who is killing people."

John had very little respect for the answer that Sam gave, so he responded by saying very directly, "Things are not fine, and no matter what decisions are made concerning the Medical Project, no one should take things into their own hands and begin killing people."

Sam also, with an upset tone, said, "John, you and the team can leave right now if you are accusing me of these killings."

John responded by saying, "I have been asked to solve this problem and have some more questions I need to have answered."

Sam said, "Ask your questions, and I will try to answer them the best I can."

John then asked, "Have you contacted anyone in Brazil or in the agency other than Kate and me?

He said, "No to both your questions." John decided to stop asking questions at that point since he knew he was lying. He did see Jim's administrative assistant's number on his pad and also knew from the investigative work that Sam or someone in his company was making calls to Brazil.

John then said, "Thank you, Sam. I have no more questions right now, but would you mind if Juan Carlos and Fabio search your facility to see if someone in your organization could be causing these problems."

"Not without a search warrant."

"OK, we will come back later with a search warrant."

Sam responded and was very upset when he said, "Fine, have them come back."

John and the team left the board room. Both teams were upset when they parted. After they left the building and they got back into the car.

Everyone could see that John was upset. He looked at both Fabio and Juan Carlos and said, "I will be going back to the agency tomorrow. I believe Sam is the person responsible for the killings but want to get more information. I need you guys to stay here until I can get a search warrant. Then I will have you lead a search of Sam's business. It is late, so I think I will go back to the hotel and hit the sack. You guys must be tired also after that long flight."

Juan Carlos responded, "We were hoping you would say that. We are tired too. I think it is a room service night."

John was tired, but he did call Kate and said, "I saw Doris's name and phone number on Sam's pad. Do you think Doris could be the leak in the agency?

Kate said, "I had lunch with Doris, and I am sure that Doris was not leaking anything. She comes from a great family and would not want to embarrass her mom or dad. She is also very loyal to the agency."

"How did your lunch go with her today?"

"I purposely talked about non-work things. She has a boyfriend she has been going with for about a year who she really loves. He is rich and from Dallas but spends a lot of time in Washington."

There was silence on the phone for a few seconds. John got a worried look on his face and was hoping that what he was thinking was not true, but he needed to ask, "Kate, I hope this is not true. Do you think her boyfriend could be Sam?"

There was silence on the other end of the line for a while, and then Kate said, "I am concerned. I think it could be him. I will call Jim as soon as I hang up. We will see if he can locate her, but since it is ten, it may be too late to do anything at this point."

John responded, "I hope we are wrong this time. I will see you at the agency in the afternoon. I am keeping Juan Carlos and Fabio here just so they can search and get more information from Sam or his company."

Kate does not call Jim at his house during the night too often, but as soon she hung up with John, she picked up the phone again and, with a voice that had a sense of urgency, got Jim on the phone and said, "Jim, John and I are concerned that Doris could be leaking things to Sam Jacob. She is probably doing it unknowingly.

We believe she may have known this person for about a year, and he could be getting this information by just looking at calendars of people through Doris since Doris does have everyone's calendar. I am worried because she could be meeting with him now. At lunch, she told me she was meeting with her boyfriend. Since he now knows we suspect he is behind all the killings, he may try to burn his bridges so we cannot get evidence against him."

"You were right to call me, Kate. Let me get security on this immediately and see if they can get into her desk to see if she made a note on where she could be now. Kate, do you think you could give her parents a call to see if they know where she has gone. I would not alarm them until we can confirm our suspicion. Let's get back together in half an hour."

"OK, I will call you in half an hour."

Doris and her mother, Janis, were very close. They used to go out for lunch two times per week. Also, Doris and Janis both went to the same college. Doris was Janis's only child. Her parents gave her the down payment on her first house.

When Kate talked with Janis, Janis said, "I know exactly where Doris is staying in Annapolis." She gave Kate the address and also said, "I know about Doris's boyfriend, but for some reason, she never brought him home for dinner since he always seemed very busy. She would always tell me that he was a man of the world and very rich. When they were together, it seemed like they would always be flying places in his jet or meeting in Annapolis."

Kate did not wait for the half-hour but immediately called Jim and said, "I know where they are, and from the description her mother gave me, it could be Sam Jacob."

"OK, Kate, can you come with me tonight to see if we can get Doris?"

"Yes, I want to help."

"OK, be dressed in about thirty minutes, and I'll have your security agent take you to the local airport, and we will pick you up in a helicopter."

"I will be there waiting."

A car with two security guards picked Kate up at her house, and with security guards that were guarding her, all went to the airport. Jim, Kate, and several security people went aboard the two helicopters and headed toward Annapolis and to the address given by Janis.

As they approached the address where Doris was meeting her boyfriend, they noticed an open field next to the house that Doris's mother gave Kate. Both helicopters landed in the open field.

The moment the helicopters landed, the security guards, which had automatic weapons, left the helicopters and ran to the house. Jim and Kate followed slowly behind the guards just in case there was gunfire. Jim and Kate stayed outside the house waiting, for the all-clear.

After about thirty seconds, a guard came out with a very depressed look on his face and said, "We are too late."

Kate cried out, "Oh no!"

Jim and Kate then walked into the cabin, and they saw Doris there on the ground. Her throat was cut, and she was dead. The security people immediately took Jim and Kate out of the house and called the local police.

They said, "Sorry, sir. Some of us will stay here until the local police arrive. We need to make sure we get any evidence we can and do not want to disturb the crime area. Why don't you and Kate head back to your homes and get some rest?"

Jim was sorrowful and responded to the guard and said, "Thank you. Do what needs to be done here. I want to find the person who did this and when you talk to the police, let them know how important this is. Kate and I will head back to Washington. We want to break the news to her parents face to face as soon as possible and before it leaks out over the news. Please give me an update tomorrow."

Kate and Jim headed back to the helicopter with two guards, got in and took off, for Doris's parents' house. The pilot had been on the walkie-talkie with people that knew exactly how to get to the house.

Doris's parents lived on a farm, so they knew it would not be difficult to land close to their house. When they arrived at the house, Janis and her husband Joe had heard the helicopter and were on their porch. They lived on a ranch about sixty miles from Washington. As Kate and Jim approached the porch, Janis knew there was something wrong. Jim then spoke, "A terrible thing has happened. Someone has killed Doris. I am so sorry. We will find the person who did this, believe me."

Joe took Janis in his arms, and they just hugged and broke down crying. This was a blow that Janis and Joe could not take. Doris was a daughter that everyone would want to have. She did well in school and always had many friends.

Kate hugged both of them and also started crying. Just over the last few days, Doris had become one of Kate's best friends. Also, when Kate thought of Doris, she often saw her own daughter.

They were both thirty years old and beautiful in every way.

Jim told Joe and Janis, "I don't want you to worry about anything. The agency will take care of all funeral arrangements. I also want both of you to call on Kate or me for anything you may need to get you through this terrible tragedy.

Kate went on to say, "You must think of the precious time you had with your daughter. Most people never get to experience someone like that, and you had her for thirty years. Would you like to stay with John and me tonight?

"No, thank you, Kate. Thank you both for coming here and also trying to save my daughter."

"I will call you tomorrow."

As soon as Kate got home, she debated whether she should call John immediately. She decided to let him sleep and call him in the morning.

DINNER WITH DORIS'S PARENTS

Kate set her alarm so she would wake up before John left the hotel. She wanted to catch him and give him the news about Doris. She was able to get him on the phone and said, "John, I have some bad news to give you. Doris was killed last night. Jim and I tried to get to her before she was killed, but we must have just missed the killer. We were at her cabin in Annapolis within an hour after our call. There was nothing we could do."

"Kate, you must be exhausted. You were probably up all night."

"Yes, it all would have been worth it if we could have gotten to her in time."

"Did you tell her parents?"

"Yes, Jim and I flew to their farm last night. They were devastated. I told them we would call them today."

"Excellent idea! You should let Jim know we will call on them, and if the police would like to join us, they are welcome. I would like to find the person that could have killed her. Based on our call last night, I think it was Sam Jacob, but maybe we can get more information from them on her boyfriend."

"I will call her and see if they want to talk about the person that could have killed their daughter. I believe they would want to be involved in finding the killer of their daughter."

"OK, I will see you soon."

Kate called Jim to let him know that both John and she were going to plan to spend some time at Doris's parents' house to discuss funeral arrangements and also see if they could find a link between Sam Jacob and their daughter. Jim thought that was a good idea.

She then called Janis and briefed her on the funeral arrangements that were made. After that discussion, she then changed the subject and asked Janis, "Can John and I spend some time with you and Joe so we can get to the bottom of who could have killed her.

Janis responded, "Please come to the house for dinner. You should plan to arrive at 4 p.m. so we can talk before dinner."

John arrived at his house and immediately showered and changed into some clean clothes. Then he and Kate got in a car with two security guards and headed to Joe and Janis's home. When they arrived, John put his arms around Joe and then Janis and said, "When our daughter Katelin was close to dying of cancer, I felt an empty feeling, which you must be feeling now. The only thing you can say now is that she is in a better place. I know she was your best friend and also a beautiful, intelligent person."

Kate then said, "John and I are so happy that we did get to know her."

You could tell that both Joe and Janis were doing a lot of crying, but Joe said, "We both want to find our daughter's killer. We did talk to the police today, and now I want to let you know what we know. It may help catch the person that did this to our daughter. I think if we focus on this, it may also help get through this period of the mourning."

John then asked, "Did Doris ever mention her boyfriend's name?"

Janis responded, "His name is Michael Smith. She also said that he had his own plane, and they would travel a great deal whenever Doris could get away."

John asked, "Did you ever see him, or do you know anything about him?"

Joe responded, "We never saw him. He works with a medical company. In fact, he may be the president. He is older than Doris. He is from Dallas and is very rich. That is really all we know about him."

Janis then said, "I want to thank the agency for making all the funeral arrangements for us. My understanding is that everything will be held at the funeral parlor, and the car will pick us up tomorrow at the house. This really takes a lot off our minds. Joe has already made arrangements for us to get away after the funeral and try to get through these next few weeks. Come on and sit down. We can have dinner."

During dinner, they talked about different things they all did with Doris.

When John and Kate were about to leave, Kate said, "I am leaving numbers where you can reach us. If you ever want someone to talk with, then give us a call. As soon as you get back from your trip, we want you to come to our house. We will keep you updated on what we find out."

On the way home after dinner, John said to Kate, "You realize that Michael Smith is really Sam Jacob, but there is no way to prove it at this time. The reason that Sam Jacob wanted to get rid of Doris is that all of the killings would be traced back to him once we started questioning Doris about Sam and how he could have stolen information from her. "

"You are right. She knew too much about him and also about what was going on in Jim's office, and he knew all this would have been traced back to him. She would travel with Jim most of the time, and she held everyone's calendars. It would be easy for Sam to get a copy of the calendars of everyone in the department once he knew where they were kept by Doris."

"I believe that Joe is right about focusing on finding the killer of Doris. It will help us all get through this period of mourning. You know I can't believe that Sam would kill someone. He was so brilliant. I guess he lived on the edge and just went over that edge this time. We will get him."

THE FUNERAL

John and Kate woke up at six and went for their run. There were two guards that followed in a car. They talked throughout their run about the funeral, work, and Katelin. It was a beautiful day, so they stopped in the middle of their run and enjoyed the moment as they just sat on a bench overlooking a lake.

After the run, they got ready for the funeral. John and Kate did not speak too much when they were dressing. It was a sad moment. They just could not get the thought out of their head that they would not see Doris ever again.

She was so bright, so vibrant, and just a great person. All of a sudden, the doorbell rang, and Kate said, "Just a moment." Then turned to John and said, "We better get a move on it."

John nodded and said, "I am ready. I will go to the door and see who it is." John went to the front door and asked, "Who is it."

"Your car is ready, sir. When you are ready, I will be waiting in the car."

"Thank you. We should be just a moment."

John yelled out to Kate, "It's the car driver."

"OK, John, I am coming."

Moments later, Kate appeared in a black dress. Her black hair, brown eyes, and beautiful figure still catch John's eye every time he sees her.

Kate smiled and wiggled a little and said, "OK handsome, put your eyes back in your head and let's go.

Kate and John went out the door. The two guards at the door

followed them into the car. The car went directly to the funeral home, and there must have been two hundred people. It was one of the biggest funerals that John and Kate have ever seen.

Jim was with Doris's parents consoling them. John and Kate went over to them. Kate wrapped her arms around Janis, and John gave Joe a hug. Then they switched, and Kate gave Joe a hug, and Janis gave John a hug.

Joe and Janis had all of their family at the funeral, and this was a time for them to get together. Jim, John, and Kate then went to one end of the funeral parlors and began talking about the good times they had with Doris.

Then the subject switched. John, Jim, and Kate all wanted to catch the killer, so John said to Jim, "We need to put a trace on everything that Sam is doing. We need to trace all of his phone calls and also any travel being done by his plane. We should also get a search warrant and have Juan Carlos and Fabio search his house and offices. We should also pick him up for questioning. We now have enough justification based on calls they made to Rio de Janeiro and his possible association with Doris."

"I agree. I will get things started tonight. We will get our Dallas team, plus Juan Carlos and Fabio working over the weekend. Sam's team will not expect things to happen on the weekend. Let's try to get back together first thing Monday morning and see what they find."

A DAY OF REST

John woke up at six and asked Kate what he asks almost every morning when they are together, "Kate, you want to go for a run?" She turned over and, half-awake, said, "Today, we are going to do something different." After staying in bed and making love, they later decided to go out for breakfast and a drive. Before leaving, they did call Katelin, but she had plans with her friends for the day and could not join them.

It was not going to be like their usual breakfast on weekends because there were going to be two bodyguards and a car. John let the guards know what their plans were so they could prepare and follow them.

Breakfast was great. John and Kate always had breakfast out when they were dating, and with just the two of them, this was like dating again. After breakfast, Kate suggested an early show at the movie located in the mall close to their house. When John and Kate usually go to a movie at the mall, they window shop until the movie starts. She knows that John really likes his bag of popcorn and a diet cola with a good movie.

The movie they go to, according to John, is like the movie they will have in heaven for those who like movies. It has huge screens, seats that rock, and surround sound. It puts you in another world and allows you to forget about any problems you may have. The car driver did drive them to the mall, and they got there early and started walking around the mall.

As they were walking, they noticed Katelin at the far end of the mall. She was so beautiful she could pass for a model. They walked a little faster to catch up with her. Of course, the guards were behind them and were wondering what was going on.

Katelin made a turn into the food court area, so they walked a little faster. They got to the food court area and looked all around, but Katelin had disappeared.

Kate and John then turned around and started to walk back to the movie, and they heard. "Mommy! Daddy! What are you two doing here?"

It was their daughter. A tear came to their eyes. Kate was too shocked to say anything because of the funeral she was at yesterday, and then seeing their daughter made them feel thankful to have her.

John turned to their daughter and said, "We are so happy to see you."

Katelin turned to her mom, hugged her, and said, "I love you guys. So you like the pants set. Well, I got it at the petite department of Macy's. They have some left."

Kate turned to John and said, "You know where we are going after the movie."

"John smiled and said, "I bet we are going to Macy's."

Katelin then said with a sense of urgency, "Ok, you guys, I got to get going. I have a lunch engagement."

Kate looked and asked the question, "Anyone you want to introduce to your mom and dad."

Katelin smiled and said, "You guys will be the first to know if anything gets serious. I will talk to you on the phone tonight."

Kate and John then headed off to the movie. John got his popcorn and cola. Kate looked at him while he was sitting there, and he looked like a little kid having fun.

After the movie, they made a trip to Macy's, and Kate went straight to the petite department. She went to the manager and tried to describe the pantsuit she wanted, and then after a few minutes, the manager pulled out a pantsuit behind the counter. It was exactly what she wanted. Kate had a look of surprise and said, "How did you know what I wanted and how come you have my size behind the counter."

The manager smiled and said, "Do you both know a pretty young lady with long light brown wavy hair?"

John and Kate just looked at each other, smiled, and almost said this at the same time, "We are the luckiest people in the world."

Katelin was a very special person. She enjoyed giving and making people happy. Of course, Kate bought the outfit. They both went home and just relaxed and watched TV. They also had dinner at home. John did the cooking.

SHOWDOWN IN PORTO ALEGRE

When John and Kate woke up Sunday morning, they both went for their run and then headed to work in the car with the two security guards. As soon as they arrived, they went to Jim's office. Jim was on the phone, and he motioned that they should get together in an hour. They were all working a 7-day week until they caught the person that killed Doris.

Since Jim had gotten the search warrants for Juan Carlos and Fabio to search Sam Jacob's office and home and they started the search, John decided to call Juan Carlos and Fabio during that hour to get an update from them on the status of their search. During that time, Kate needed to check her mail and take care of some office items.

Everyone got back together after an hour, and Jim said, "Sam has disappeared. Since he flies his own planes, it would be hard to find him.

Our agents in Dallas had gone directly to Sam's offices in Dallas and his home this weekend. It is my understanding that they brought Juan Carlos and Fabio with them while performing the search. They were told to search all the files for links to Doris's death and the deaths in Rio."

John responded, "It is clear that Sam was going to try to stop the project from seeing the light of day and would try to do it while out of the country. It will be difficult to stop him as long as he stays away from us and as long as we do not get specific proof that links him to a crime."

Jim responded, "Right now, we were still collecting data and running tests on things found at the Annapolis cabin. Sam told some company leaders that he would be gone for a while but to continue running the business without him."

John responded about the conversation he had with Fabio and Juan Carlos this morning, "Fabio and Juan Carlos did find some papers in the Dallas office, and they had information that would indicate that the Mob boss in Rio de Janeiro was in communication with Sam and doing business with him.

The name of the person that Sam was doing business with was Paulo Costo. Paulo was dealing drugs and prostitution. He also had hundreds of killers working for him throughout Brazil. They were also able to get Sam's calendar off his computer, which indicated that he was traveling to Annapolis, Rio de Janeiro, and other countries that had people killed like Paris, Tokyo, Singapore, England, and Mexico."

Jim said, "The other item that concerned us was that in addition to those countries, there were three other countries on the list. The countries were Brazil, Germany, and Australia. I knew about Brazil, and they thought they had the right security measures in place to prevent problems in Brazil, but the other countries were new news."

Kate said, "I will immediately contact people still working on the program in those countries and ensure those people have security."

Jim said with a look of disappointment, "Finding Sam is going to be very difficult. He is rich, has his means of transportation, and owns several islands. I have our satellite systems looking for him and his plane."

John was more enthusiastic when he said, "Jim, it looks like we have enough information to go after the mob boss in Brazil. I think I will go down there and work with them on the questioning of the mob boss and his team. If we can capture him or his people alive, we may be able to get them to talk and tell us where Sam is located. While I am doing that, you can continue to work here to see if you can track down Sam."

Kate said, "Do they know where the mob boss is located?"

John responded, "They believe he is hiding in a city called Porto Alegre. Porto Alegre is a small city in the south part of Brazil, very close to the Argentina border. Both Fabio and Juan Carlos are on a plane to Porto Alegre. The Chief of Police is already there with over a hundred-armed officers. The area where the mob boss is located is in an area outside of town and heavily wooded."

Jim asked, "Do you think they need any help from us? We can have Stealth Fighters standing by just in case they have problems."

John responded, "This could escalate, and I believe we should have Stealth Fighters ready to help with this raid if necessary. They would be called upon and fly into Brazil air space only when called upon by the Brazil Government."

Jim responded, "I will make arrangements with the Brazil Government and our armed forces. Did they tell you how they plan to get this mob boss?"

"It was decided that the raid would take place tonight, so they can catch him before he tries to move to another place. They plan to use ground forces."

"Tell them that we would like someone to keep us posted in our war room on what is happening so we will be able to send in Stealth Fighters if needed."

"I will get in touch with Juan Carlos and Fabio when their plane lands and make the arrangements on that end. One other thing, Jim, if we do capture the mob boss, I will want to go down there for the questioning."

Jim responded, "Let's see what happens, and then we will make that decision later. It looks like this may be a long night."

John did get in touch with Juan Carlos, Fabio, and the Chief of Police. They all agreed the two war rooms would be set up. One of the war rooms would be in Porto Alegre and the other one in Washington so the two groups could talk. The raid on the mob boss's camp would start that night at nine since many of them may be having dinner at that time.

That night at about eight-thirty, the two war rooms were up and running. Juan Carlos, running the communication lines on that end, said, "Everything is set up on this end, and ground troupes will begin invasion in 30 minutes. Are the Stealth in position so they can get here if we need them?"

Jim told John to man the war room on the U.S. end just in case Portuguese translation was needed. John started the war room conversation by saying, "It is nine, and the Stealth is right off the coast and can get to your position quickly."

Juan Carlos started describing the invasion by saying, "They are going in now. They are destroying the mob's boss defenses. It looks like this will be over soon. The mob boss had some helicopters that were hidden, and he was sending them into the battle. We are beginning to send in our helicopters. Oh my God, they have more helicopters than we do. Our helicopters are being shot down. We only have a few helicopters left, and they are now going after the ground troupes."

Juan Carlos commented that they needed to discuss something. There was silence for about thirty seconds on the communication line. Then Juan Carlos came on the line, and you could tell there was some disappointment in the way things were going. There was also a sense of urgency in his voice when he said, "John, we need the Stealth Fighters."

"OK, Juan Carlos, here they come. They will be there in less than a minute."

"Tell them to hurry. If the mob helicopters land and pick up the mob boss and his people, then it will be hard to get the mob boss or anyone else alive. All our helicopters have been shot down. They are now killing police with their rockets and guns. The ground troupes were no match for the helicopters."

"The Stealth fighters should be arriving soon."

"OK, the Stealth fighters are here. The helicopters are trying to attack the Stealth but are being shot down one by one. They are destroying the mob helicopters. It has only been one minute, and there are only two mob helicopters left and they are trying to get away. The Stealth just caught them and shot them down. The good news is that none of the helicopters were able to land and pick up the mob bosses.

The mob now has no defenses. The ground troupes are now going in, and there is no resistance. The Stealth Fighters are watching at a distance."

There was a silence on the line for about a minute, and then John said, "Juan Carlos is there any word on the mob boss and his people? Have they captured anyone?

"Nothing yet, but from what I am hearing, they have found the building the mob boss is in, and they are about to break down the door. They have asked them to surrender."

There was a silence on the line for about thirty seconds, and then Juan Carlos came on the line, and with great enthusiasm, said, "The mob boss and his people have their hands up, and they are being taken into custody."

"OK, this is great news. We are bringing the Stealth Fighters home."

"OK! The Stealth fighters have saved the day. Thank the pilots for me."

Juan Carlos said with great enthusiasm, "John, it is confirmed we have the mob boss, and we are leaving tonight to bring him back to Rio de Janeiro for questioning."

John responded, "Tell your team we are all proud of them. Just a second, Juan Carlos, I need to put you on mute for a minute."

John then put on the mute button so no one could hear and then looked at Jim and said, "Should Kate and I go there for the questioning? I think if both of us are there, then we have a better chance of getting Sam Jacob linked to the project. We also will be able to make sure we restart the medical project in Brazil correctly."

Jim responded, "John, are you sure this is a good idea?" I cannot afford to put both of you in harm's way."

"It should be safe in Brazil now that we have the mob boss and all his people, plus we need to make some progress on the program while we are getting the killers."

Kate responded, "It will be OK, Jim."

"OK, but this time I will have the agency jet take you down and a helicopter meet you at the airport and take both of you to our offices in the city."

Kate responds, "OK, let's do it."

John looked at Jim and nodded his head, and Jim looked at John and nodded back. Then John took off the mute button and said, "Juan Carlos, Kate, and I want to be there for the mob boss questioning on Tuesday. I want to make sure we have the link to Sam Jacob. Please make sure that Caesar is there for the questioning. Also, I want Kate to be there to make sure we get the project restarted properly.

We will be taking the agency jet to Rio and then the helicopter to the agency."

"OK, John, I look forward to seeing you both here on Tuesday. Thank you for your support."

Everyone hung up, and then John and Kate turned to Jim and said with a sense of urgency, "We better be heading home to pack and take care of somethings so we can get in the air sometime Monday night."

Jim looked at both of them and said, "I do not want you to be taking any chances. I will get the pilots and also get the agency jet ready. I will also make sure security is with you, and the helicopter is ready in Rio de Janeiro. I will work on that tomorrow."

"Thanks, Jim. We will be careful and keep you informed."

John and Kate left the agency quickly and got into the car with two bodyguards. They went home, called Katelin to let her know they would be leaving Monday afternoon. They both went to bed and slept in on Monday and woke up at about 2 p.m. They then started to get packed, and got into the car that was taking them to the airport. When they arrived at the airport, the agency jet was ready to go, and they took off.

Questioning in Rio de Janeiro Lost a Day in Travel

John, Kate, and their two bodyguards arrived at the agency at 10 in the morning the next day because they were not able to leave until Monday night. They lost a day with all the travel. Juan Carlos worked with Kate when she was on the project, so when she walked into the office with John, Juan Carlos ran up to Kate, put his arms around her, and kissed her on her cheek, saying, "Kate, it is so nice to see you again. I am so thankful for your help. You both saved my life and my family's life."

John had warned Kate on their first trip to Latin America to be aware that they would give her a kiss. John thought they especially did it when it was a beautiful lady. He then hugged John saying, "Thanks again, John."

Kate looked over to John and gave him a big smile. This was worth every sacrifice she had made on this project. John wanted her to have this feeling, and it was one of the main reasons for having her on the trip.

Kate then responded to Juan Carlos, saying, "OK, let's question this guy and get to the leader of these killings and the killing of Caesar's son. Kate, you can stay in this room with the Police Chief and Caesar. You can hear and see everything that goes on in the room with the mob leader and everything will be translated, but they cannot see or hear you."

Juan Carlos, John, and a security guard then went into a room that contained the Mob leader and his lawyer. As they went into the room, Juan Carlos was angry and said, "We have evidence from your people that you ordered the attack on John and the US Ambassador. We also have evidence from Sam Jacob's office that you are responsible for killings here in Brazil."

The lawyer then said, "I would like to see this evidence." Juan Carlos then showed him documents from Sam's offices."

The lawyer asked to talk with his client in private for ten minutes. They then took them to a private room, and when they returned, the attorney said, "What is the deal?"

Juan Carlos then said, "We want to know exactly who the people were that went to Caesar Ponte's house and killed his son. Then we want to know the name of the person that was directing you. We believe that person is Sam Jacob, but we want it in writing from you. We also need to know where Sam Jacob is now. Additionally, we want to know what other plans you have for stopping the project."

This type of questioning went back and forth for about three hours until finally, the mob lawyer said, "If we can give you this information, then what can you give us?"

"For that information, you can spend the rest of your life in prison with no parole. If you do not give us the information, then you will get death."

The Mob Leader then turned to his attorney, shook his head yes; and said, "OK, I can give you all this information. We have a deal."

Juan Carlos and John then left the room and went into the room containing Kate, Caesar, and the Chief of Police. As they left, others came into the room and began getting the details needed from the mob boss.

Juan Carlos and John entered the room where Caesar, Kate, and the Police Chief were staying. When they got in the room, everyone started hugging and shaking hands and congratulating each other. It was an unforgettable moment.

Juan Carlos then said, "I think we can restart the program and focus on things that can get the Medical Project running again. John, can you or Kate work with me for a couple of days so we can make sure we get things going in the right direction."

John then responded, "Juan Carlos can you join Kate and me on the plane trip back to Washington. I believe with the mob boss captured. You and your team should be safe. Kate can work with you for a while now, but I also want you to work with Paul Darma. You remember Paul Darma, don't you?

He will be working with Kate in putting together the design that we want to use for the remainder of the medical projects around the world. I will head back to Washington with you, but I will be working with Jim in finding the island in the Caribbean where this mob boss says Sam is located."

"I will do it. When do you plan on going back?"

"As soon as you pack, we will take the helicopter to the airport and then the agency plane that is waiting for us."

"OK, I will be back here about 7 p.m."

While waiting for Juan Carlos, John called Jim and gave him an update, to which Jim responded with great enthusiasm, "Outstanding, you guys did great. Based on what you told me, I will start trying to get some satellite information to locate airstrips on a Caribbean Island that could land a 747 aircraft."

"OK, Jim, but since we will not be getting back until around noon tomorrow, I will see you Thursday morning.

"Be careful and try to get some rest! Until we get this guy, you and Kate are still in danger. I will have three security guards meet you at your house."

The trip back home was uneventful, which is what you want. On the way back, Jim called them on the plane. He had a very positive tone when he said, "We were able to locate the island in the Caribbean. The island is heavily fortified."

John suggested, "Since Paul Darma and I have worked with Sam before, it may be best for the both of us to head out to the island on Thursday. Maybe we can get him to give himself up, which could save lives."

"I do not think he is going to give himself up, but it is worth a try. I will start making plans to capture him and ensure no one leaves the island. It will take me until Thursday to get all the forces in place."

DANGER AT HOME

When John and Kate finally got home, it was 11 p.m. Juan Carlos had a security guard with him from Rio. John and Kate were met at the airport with two security guards and a car. John and Kate invited Juan Carlos to stay with them at their house, but Juan Carlos wanted to give John and Kate some time alone, so he told them he would stay at a hotel.

They knew that they had this problem solved and all that remained was a raid on Sam's Island. When John and Kate arrived at their house, Bill and three other security guards met them at the house.

When they got into the house, the phone was ringing. Kate picked the phone up and said, "Hello."

"Hello, Mom, how are things going?"

"Things are fine. This is almost over, and we can start doing real work pretty soon."

"How are you feeling?"

"I have a little pain, but probably due to all the tests they are still doing to verify the cancer is still gone."

"How about if I come over tonight?"

"That would be great. It will be a girl's night. I can bring you up to date on what is going on at work."

"See you in about an hour."

"John, I am heading over to Katelin's for the night."

"OK, have fun! Tell Katelin I love her and will be seeing more of her in a few weeks. I want you to take three of these guards with you."

"No, I will take two, and you keep two."

"OK, I will see you at work tomorrow morning."

Bill and another guard stayed with John. Bill was in the house, and the other guard stayed outside. John was working on his computer when Bill asked, "What are you doing?"

"I do this every chance I get. I continue to do research on cancer."

"I thought your daughter was in remission."

"She is, but I want to be prepared just in case something changes. It is getting late, and my mind is turning to mush. I am not able to concentrate. I did not get much sleep on the plane, so I think I will go to bed early tonight. See you in the morning."

That night John had difficulty sleeping. He kept thinking about his daughter and wife. After about two hours of sleeping, he woke up went to the bathroom, and went into the kitchen for a snack and some water. Bill was in the kitchen, so John said, "Hey, guy. I woke up, so I thought I would grab a snack."

Then John looked out the kitchen window and said, "Bill, where is the other guard? He usually sits at the table in the backyard."

Bill picked up his walkie-talkie and said, "Joe, come in."

There was no answer. Then John noticed some men in dark uniforms cutting across his yard. He whispered to Bill, "Call headquarters and tell them to send people to Katelin's apartment and also this house. Tell them we have some people running around in our backyard, and the guard outside is not responding. It looked like they were about to break into this house."

"OK, they got my call and are sending people. We just need to hold them off until they get to us. They are also going to Katelin's apartment."

"John, get your gun. They are starting to rush the house."

"Bill, they just fired some canisters of gas in the house. We may have to get out of the house. They will probably rush the house as soon as the gas gets to us. I notice they are putting on their gas masks."

"John, take cover. They are starting to come in the door."

At that moment, some people came through the door and started shooting their machine guns in all directions. John and Bill fired at the men, killing two of them.

The people kept coming in the front door and windows. Bill and John killed three more of them. Bill then said, "We better get out of here, now! We will have a better chance outside."

John responded, "I run here every day, and if we can get to the park two blocks away, then I believe we will be OK. Follow me!"

John, shot his gun at a glass sliding door leading to the pool and backyard. The glass shattered. He then crawled to the door and then stood up, and ran out the door. Bill was right behind him. There was gunfire all around him, but they were able to get to the street quickly. From that point, he started running to the parking area. As they were running down the street, they noticed about ten people running after them and some other people getting into a truck. They were running as fast as they could, but they were still a block from the woods.

Just as they entered the woods, they noticed two helicopters and several cars coming straight at them. He hit the ground, and as the helicopters passed over him, he noticed they were from the US. They proceeded to blow up the truck and kill the other ten people. In 30 seconds, it was all over, and the helicopters landed. John immediately got in a helicopter and asked them to take him and Bill to Katelin's house.

In less than two minutes, they were at Katelin's apartment, and as John stepped out of the helicopter, he noticed everything was calm and quiet. The guards were already at the apartment. It was now midnight, and John entered the apartment door. He opened the door and said, "Thank God everything is OK."

Kate said, "The guards told us what happened. Are you OK?"

John responded, "Bill and I are OK, but I believe a guard was killed."

Katelin said, "Daddy, I am really worried about everything that is happening. I love you both so much. I don't want to lose you. This is more than just the medical project."

"You are right, Katelin. This is more than your mom, and I signed up for when this began. We are close to getting done with the dangerous part. I want you and your mom to have this present. I have been carrying them with me since I came back from Rio de Janeiro."

He handed them each a stone. The stones were a thousand years old. With a tear in his eye said, "I love you both, and as the stone says, I will be with you and take care of you for a thousand years."

Katelin and Kate both put their arms around John and gave him a kiss, and both said, "We love you." They decided to stay at Katelin's apartment for the remainder of the night and get some rest before going to work.

PREPARING FOR THE ATTACK

They all woke up at about 8 Thursday morning. John and Kate had a change of clothes that they always left at Katelin's, so they all got dressed and all went into Katelin's kitchen and sat at the table, and started talking about items that were going on at Katelin's work. Everyone had just finished their coffee, and Katelin said, "Are you guys, OK? What are you going to do now?"

Then Kate looked her daughter straight in the eye and said, "We are OK! We are now going to get the guy that is trying to stop The Medical Project!"

They all stood up and went out the door. Two of the guards were there to follow Katelin to work. John and Kate's car and an extra agency car were also there to take John and Kate to work. Two of the guards went in the car, and there was a car that followed with two more guards.

John and Kate rushed to the war room that was a command center for the raid on Sam's Island. When John and Kate got to the command center, Juan Carlos, Paul Darma, Jim, and some people from the armed forces were all sitting down. Jim started the discussion by saying, "John, both you and Paul know Sam Jacob from past jobs, don't you?"

John responded, "Yes, we both tried to convince Sam to get involved with the Medical Project, but he wanted to go a different way. Do you want us to try and make contact with him? We may be able to get him to make a mistake if we can get him to talk with us."

Jim said with a very serious look on his face, "John, I believe I want you and Paul to be in the war room in the Caribbean on the Air Craft Carrier. We will fly you and Paul to a carrier we have in the Caribbean Islands. Kate, I want you to run the war room here with me. The objective will be to confirm he is on the island we think he is on and then get him."

"We also want to complete this with minimal deaths to our people. The satellite view indicated that the 747 plane that Sam uses landed on the island and never left, so they are fairly certain that Sam is still on the island. There is a big hanger that houses the 747. The other item that the satellite showed was heavy armament, antiaircraft, and something that looked similar to a rocket that could launch a satellite. This rocket could then carry a nuclear weapon. This is what concerns people in Washington the most."

John then said, "If we can communicate with Sam and demonstrate he does not have a chance if he goes to war with us, then maybe he will give himself up."

Jim responded, "Don't count on it. He has some plan that he is keeping to himself, which we have not figured out. Based on the firepower on that island, I have asked that three Stealth aircraft be ready at strike time.

The strike will take place tomorrow night at eleven. We will fly you to the aircraft carrier tomorrow morning. The plan tomorrow will be to make contact with Sam on the Island tomorrow night at nine. The main object, as we said, is to verify he is on the island. If he gives himself up, we will call off the Stealth Fighters. At eleven, we will bomb the island until they give up or until we know that they cannot defend themselves, and then we will send in ground troupes."

For the remainder of the day at work, everyone worked on checking out the systems in the war rooms, doing verification checks on Sam Jacob's location, and getting everything set up for the attack tomorrow.

After work, the car took John and Kate home, and there were several security guards that went with them and stayed at the house. Once they got into the house, John said, "Well, this stage of the project is coming to an end. I will be glad when we can get this stage behind us."

Kate responded, "Me too! I do not want you taking any unnecessary chances."

"I understand. Do you want to celebrate tonight with a pizza?"

"Pizza sounds good to me. Let the guards know what we are doing and ask if they would like some also."

John checked with the guards, and they all declined, so John ordered for his wife and him. When the pizza came, the driver came to the door and said, "I have never seen anything like this. What is going on? There are so many bodyguards and police."

John responded, "It does look exciting, but it should be over soon." John gave him the money and went into the house with two medium pizzas.

John said to Kate, "I got you a cheese pizza with no sauce, and I got myself a ham, cheese, and pineapple pizza."

"Sounds good. I'll pour the wine. Let's sit down and eat."

"I do not anticipate any problems tomorrow. I believe this will be over quickly."

"The thing that worries me the most is the same thing that is concerning Washington. If there is an atomic warhead that explodes in the area, then that would not be good."

"I am sure they have thought about this, and the aircraft carrier is far enough away so that if that size bomb goes off, we will be out of range."

"Well, let's make sure you are right about this tomorrow."

John said, "I want to make a toast. This is to our love and happiness."

"I love you, John. Let's make sure we get to bed early. We will have a long day tomorrow."

"Kate, let's get Katelin on the speaker phone and let her know we will not be reachable tomorrow."

"OK, but we will not be able to give her any details."

John dialed Katelin's number and got her on the speaker phone. "Hello, Katelin. Mom and dad are here, and we have you on the speaker phone. How are you doing?"

"I am doing fine. Are you guys still in harm's way?"

"They have us pretty well protected now."

"They have also doubled the guards they have on me. I saw something in the paper on Doris. What happened?"

Kate spoke up, saying, "We did not want to worry you, honey, so we did not tell you about that since you really did not know Doris. She was working for the agency. I will give you more details later."

"Well, I am worried about you guys. When will this be over?"

"Soon, we hope, and that is why your daddy and I wanted to call you. We will not be reachable tomorrow, so we don't want you to get worried if we are not home. Of course, the guards that are with you will always know how to reach us in an emergency."

"I suppose you cannot give me any details, right?"

"You are right, but we will see you the day after tomorrow."

"OK, please be very careful. Don't take any chances. I love you both very much."

John said, "Don't worry, we will be OK. We love you."

John and Kate finished the bottle of wine and went to the bedroom and made love.

ATTACK ON THE CARIBBEAN ISLAND

The next morning John woke up at 5:30 a.m. so he could get in a run before he left for the airport at 7:30 a.m. When he woke up, he asked Kate, "Do you want to go for a run?"

"I won't go for a run, but I will follow you on the bike."

"Sounds good to me. Let's get dressed, have a cup of coffee, and go."

"John then opened the door and told the guard, "Get ready because we are going for a run and bike ride. I will be running, and Kate will be following me on her bike."

"No problem, sir."

John looked out the door, and there were two motorcycles. John said, "I see you guys came prepared. Do you want some coffee?"

"No, we just had breakfast. We are OK."

John went into the house and told Kate, "They are prepared for us this morning."

During the run, you could tell the guards knew this was going to be a big day. They had two guards on motorcycles, and two others were running with us.

At 7:30 a.m., there were two cars. One took Kate to the agency, and the other took John to the airport. Kate gave John a kiss and said, "John stay out of harm's way."

When John got to the airport, Paul was waiting, and there was a jet aircraft waiting to take them to the aircraft carrier. John commented to Paul, "I bet you never thought you would be landing on an aircraft carrier when you joined this project?"

"You are right, but I knew it would be exciting since you and Kate are both on the project. Like you and Kate, I feel the best things on this project are ahead of us."

The jet took off, and it was a short flight to the carrier. When they landed, there were several people there to meet them. Many of them were people that led past battles. You could tell by the look on their faces that they were serious and ready for a battle.

One of the General's said, "John, here is how we will work this battle. You will be the decision-maker concerning if we go into battle or not, but once we engage, we will take over unless Sam wants to stop, and then it goes back to you."

"That sounds right to me. Does Jim agree?"

"Yes, we had a short meeting with him and the President's staff before we left to come here, but I wanted to make sure you were OK with that approach. Do you have any questions?"

"We do have about six hours before I have to call Sam. What do you want me to do between now and then?"

"Come down to the war room, and we will check out some items."

They walked down into a room that had a clear glass map of the world. The lighting was dimmed so that items highlighted on the clear glass map of the world could be seen. On that same glass, there was also a detailed map of the island.

The General asked John and Paul to come over to the map because he wanted to point out a few items, "As you can see, this is a detailed map of the island. We believe that Sam is located in this bunker. We will never be able to bomb him out of that bunker. It is too secure. Most of his guards are located around the bunker and also around the beach area. The hanger at the end of the runway contains the 747. It is very close to the bunker. We plan to knock out the hanger and 747 on the first run. There is also a large underground rocket that is in another bunker that we cannot knock out. Both bunkers are joined together via a tunnel. The two bunkers and tunnel cannot be knocked out by our rockets The rocket is big enough to carry a nuclear warhead, which our main worry. Altogether, he probably has over a thousand people on the island with some high-powered weapons and people that know how to use them. Another thing, there are five helicopters heavily armed near the hanger. The telephone number that he is using for incoming calls is written on this paper."

John responded, "This can be a long battle. I hope I can get him to give himself up."

The General answered, "This will not be a long battle. We have our rockets on the carrier and other ships that can knock out a great deal of what you see on this map in minutes. The Stealth will take out the remainder."

John asked, "What do we plan to do about the rocket in the bunker?"

"We will keep one Stealth Fighter in reserve to shoot down that rocket, if need be, and if he misses, we will take it out with rockets from the ship.

By the way, it is dinner time. We can continue this update over dinner. Do you want to get some dinner? We can then come back and make a call to the command center in Washington and then try to reach Sam."

"Sounds good to me. How about you, Paul?"

"Let's go. I have never had carrier food."

After dinner, they all went to separate rooms to get some rest, and then at 8:30 p.m., they all met back at the command center. John noticed as he walked in that Jim and Kate were on a video conference with the general, and their faces were on a big screen talking with the General. Paul was in a seat off to the side.

As John walked, in the general said, "John, please sit here beside me. We have been reviewing the plan we discussed earlier."

John said, "Hey, Jim and Kate. How are you holding up?"

Jim responded, "We are ready to get this done."

John then said to the general, "General do you know if Sam has a video conference center on the island? If they do, then let's try to connect to that first. Paul and I will sit at this table. Just show the table and the upper side of our body.

Let's pipe the call into Washington and also have the officer doing the dialing be in civilian clothes just in case he is seen on camera. I do not want them to know we are calling from a carrier.

The General looked at the person responsible for the video center and said, "Get the video center ready for call per John's request so we can make the call at 9 p.m."

The officer responded to the General, "Yes, sir!"

At about three minutes to 9 p.m., the officer responded, "We are ready to make the call. I would ask that the people in Washington push the mute button, so there is no background noise coming from your center."

The officer then started dialing the video conference center on the island. Someone came on the other end and said, "Hello can I help you?"

The officer responded, "Hello, we have John Colombo and Paul Darma here. They wish to speak with Sam Jacob."

There was no one in the picture and nothing on the other line, so John came on the line and said, "Hello, this is John Colombo, and I wish to speak to Sam Jacob. Sam, if you are there, then please pick up."

Sam came into the picture and said, "John, you are good! I did not think anyone outside my small circle of people could find me. Paul, I notice you are there also. What a team. I wish you guys would have joined my team 3 years ago. So how can I help you?"

"Sam, we have enough evidence to show that you have been responsible for trying to stop the medical project, and the police want you to give yourself up for questioning."

"John, I believe this is going to be a short conversation. Everyone knows I do not like the Medical Project. Just because someone does not like something does not mean that you can pick me up for questioning."

"Sam, we also believe you are personally responsible for Doris's death and also ordering the deaths of people working on this project in several countries."

"Do you have proof?"

"Yes, we do, but you are entitled to a fair trial, and with your money, you should turn yourself in and go to trial."

"John, I am not going to give myself up, and no one will catch me."

"Sam, don't be foolish no one will let you get away with what you have done."

"John, it was nice talking with you. I have to go now. I will not give myself up to the law for questioning."

Sam hung up, and we all hung up and then called Jim back on a separate security line. Jim came on the line and said, "OK, General, you are in charge, we know Sam is on the island, and you know what you have to do. The main objective now is to ensure nothing leaves the island, and we do not want to have a missile launch. We will start the assault on the island at eleven tonight.

John, we gave it our best shot. I believe we accomplished what we wanted to accomplish. We know he is on the island. I did not think he would give himself up."

Kate then came on and said, "Take care, you guys. Both command centers will stay online throughout the battle. General, we look to you to keep us updated as the battle continues."

Everyone took a break, and then about 10:45 p.m., they all came back to the command center. The general then took over the command center and said, "OK, are the Stealth Aircraft in position?"

A pilot from the Stealth Aircraft responds, "We are in position and ready to strike."

The General then said, "Are all the rockets from ships locked in on their targets?"

Officers from three ships then said, "All rockets are locked in on targets and ready to be fired."

The General then said, "OK, let's go to war. All rockets from ships fire. Stealth Fighter holds back until rockets have hit their targets. I will let you know when it is safe to hit your targets."

The officers from the ships responded, "All rockets fired from ships."

The General then said, "OK, we are going to wait a few minutes so we can be assured that all communications, anti-aircraft radar, and the island airport are knocked out by our rockets."

There was a camera located on the carrier that was catching all the things that were being destroyed on the island. The sky was lit up, and it looked like the biggest 4th of July celebration you have ever seen. Once all the anti-aircraft stopped and communication on the island was knocked out the General came on line and said, "Two Stealth Fighters come in and start hitting your target, and the third Stealth holds back. As soon as that is completed then I want the helicopters to start making pinpoint low level raids on the island."

A helicopter officer came on the line and said, "Helicopters are ready to take off at your command General." The Stealth Fighter pilot came on the line, "All targets hit successfully with no problems."

The General then came back on line and said, "Launch helicopters."

The helicopter pilot then came on line and said, "Six helicopters launched, and we are circling the island. All targets have been destroyed, and most of the people we see are holding up white flags."

The general then came back on line and said, "Launch ground forces."

Then an officer leading the ground troops said, "Boats and helicopters with ground troops on the way to the island."

Then all of a sudden, Kate came on the video, "We are getting a message from the satellite that a missile is about to be launched."

The general came on quickly, saying, "The third Stealth pilot, are you in position to take out the missile?"

The pilot responded, "I will be in 30 seconds."

The General then said, "Get in position quickly and arm your rocket to take this out after it is launched. We cannot take it out when it is in the bunker. Pilots can you get a look at what is being launched?"

"We can't see it since it is underground and hidden by the trees. Let me get closer. I hear a loud roar. It seems like the rocket is launching. Oh my God! It is a space shuttle."

The Stealth Fighter pilot came online and said, "General, you want me to shoot down our space shuttle." General responded, "Son, as soon as you have a shot, take it. Do not let it get into space."

"OK, General, the space shuttle is starting to lift off the island. It is clearing the trees. I am going to take my shot now. The space shuttle is hit. There is a huge explosion. Wait for a second a capsule was shot out of the shuttle and is parachuting to the ground.

The general then came online and said, "Helicopter pilot can you see if there is anything in the capsule."

"Yes, sir, there are three people in the capsule. There does not seem to be a movement. I am about to land and see if any of the people are alive."

The general came online and said, "Son, bring your video camera with you when you go to the capsule. I want to see if we can recognize any of the people in the capsule."

The helicopter landed, and as people approached the capsule, they put their cameras on each individual. John then said, "That one on the right is Sam Jacob. Are any of the people alive?"

"The helicopter pilot came online and said, "No sir, all are dead. It appears that when the explosion occurred, each person was hit with scrap metal."

Jim came on the video, "Great job, team. John and Paul, can you guys get back to Washington this morning. We have a meeting with the President first thing in the morning. General, please capture all the people on the island so we can bring them in for trial."

"We are starting the cleanup now, and we have a jet ready to take John and Paul back to Washington." The General turned to Paul and John and said, "I would go into battle with you guys anytime." John responded, "Great job General." Everyone in both command centers let out a cheer, and the celebration on the carrier went on through the night.

After the celebration, an officer brought John and Paul to the upper deck and said, "I heard about what you guys are fighting for, and I am very grateful that I was a part of making it happen. We need to get the Medical Project restarted."

Paul responded, "This was the first step. Now we can start on the next step, which is solving the medical problems we have around the world. Thank you for helping us get to the next step." John looked at Paul, and the officer gave them a big smile and said, "OK, Paul, let's get on this aircraft. The President wants to see us."

MEETING WITH THE PRESIDENT

Around seven in the morning, the aircraft that took John and Paul from the carrier to Washington airport arrived. There were helicopters waiting there to take them to the White House. They arrived at the White House at eight. The President was waiting on the steps to the White House along with the leaders in congress and the senate. Jim and Kate were waiting for John and Paul as they got off the helicopter.

As the three of them approached the President and other leaders, there was applause from all of them. The President then said, "Great job, team. You know that there are news articles on the Medical Project being published all over the world. The news of the battle is known by everyone. You are all heroes around the world. Let's get to the Oval so we can talk privately." As they walked to the Oval Office, the press was snapping pictures.

They all went into the Oval Office, and began laying out a plan on how they would continue the Project and what to say to the press. The President started by saying, "I will have to have a press conference after this meeting. I find the best thing to do is to draw a picture of what has happened and what we plan to do. John or Kate, do you have any suggestions?"

John responded, "Let them know that you were contacted by many nations concerning deaths that were occurring in the Medical Project.

You assembled a team to look into the problem and, at the same time, rallied heads of congress and the senate about restarting the Project. It was a mistake to stop the project, and the congress and senate agree, so we will, as of today, restart the Program."

Jim added, "I would also tell them that there were some people that were breaking the law and killing people that were working on the project in other countries. We had to find out who was doing this and also put a stop to it. If they ask who was doing this, then you can go into more detail concerning how we found and stopped Sam Jacob. I would also add what was done in Brazil and how we stopped the killing in Brazil."

Kate added, "You may want to say some words about the project. You should mention how we will be able to detect diseases before they turn into epidemics like AIDS and COVID and it will help doctors in their effort to diagnose illnesses.

You may want to draw an analogy to the space project of landing a person on the moon. We are setting a goal, and we are going to achieve that goal. We have a worldwide goal, and countries worldwide will work together to reach that goal."

The President turned to Kate, John, Jim and Paul and said, "Thank you all for getting us to this point. I can see why we are restarting the program and why you people are leading the Project. I will do my best to represent the Project well. The other thing I do want to add is that in two weeks, I will be coming back with an announcement of the countries that will be a part of the Medical Project. By the way, who will be contacting these countries over the next two weeks?"

Jim wanted to take that assignment and responded, "Mr. President, I will ensure all the countries that want to be included are included and will start making the calls to the Presidents in those countries."

The President responded back, "That would be great Jim, but, let me coordinate that with you since some of the countries have called me directly, and I have told them me or someone else would be calling them back."

"OK, Mr. President."

John then said, "Would it be OK if I invite some people that helped make this all happen to the announcement meeting? I believe it would also be appropriate to invite Janis and Joe. Their daughter Doris is one of the persons killed, and her death led us to Sam."

The President responded, "I want them here and would like to meet with them before the announcements. For this press conference, let's just have the people in this room involved. OK, if everyone is ready, let's go to the press conference?"

The President started off the press conference by saying, "Everyone is probably wondering why we sent an aircraft carrier to the Caribbean and also sent Stealth Fighters to Brazil and the Caribbean. Well, it was because I got calls from just about every country that was still involved in the Medical Project concerning the deaths of people still working on the project.

They were being killed by someone that did not want the Medical Project to see the light of day. Also, there was a belief that the person responsible for the killing was an American citizen.

The President then went on and told the story as they discussed it in the Oval Office. He added these comments at the end of his statement, "The people that will be leading this project going forward are John Colombo and his wife, Kate. They will report directly to Jim. John and Kate were leading it before it was stopped in the US and have helped the world. They have risked their lives to find the person who was trying to stop the project and who is responsible for the killings of people around the world.

They have gotten us this far, and with their leadership, they will make this project reach the goals we have set and make this planet a healthier place to live.

When making a toast, one of the things we usually wish for is good health. Well, we will realize this when this project is complete. See everyone in two weeks with an announcement of countries that will be participating."

The press had a few questions, which were all answered satisfactorily. Then as they all left the stage and the President said to the people who were on the stage with him, "I will see you all in a couple of days, and we will see where we are relative to the countries being signed up."

John said, "Thank you for the kind words, Mr. President." The President responded, "You all deserve them and more."

Jim told everyone, "Listen, I know we have a lot to do, but why don't you all take tomorrow off and spend some time with your family, and I will see you the day after tomorrow. John and Kate, I think I will continue the car and bodyguard until things die down a little."

Kate responded, "Thank you, Jim."

Paul said to John and Kate, "See you the day after tomorrow. You have my home number if you need me for anything." John responded, "Thanks for all your support, Paul."

John and Kate went to the car, and Bill accompanied them and said, "We have come a long way since our arrival in Rio. I will be one of the guards with you until things calm down, as Jim mentioned. My wife has already asked me if this was the project I was on, and now I can tell her. As I have said before, I am really proud to be a part of this team."

Kate responded, "We are thankful that you are with us."

Kate then turned to John and said, "John, we need to give Katelin a call."

John responded, "We told her we would be busy until today. Let's call her once we get in the car. It has a conference phone capability."

They all went to the car, and Kate hit the conference button and dialed Katelin's work number. Katelin came on the line and said, "Hello, Katelin Colombo." Her mom responded, "Hello, Katelin Colombo. This is your mom, dad, and Bill in a car on our way home giving you a call."

Katelin responded, "Mommy and Daddy, I am so proud of you guys. I knew something was up when we talked last night, but I never figured it was this big. The people at work here saw you on TV with the President, and they even brought a TV into my office, and we all watched together. Where are you guys now? Are you close to my office?"

John responded, "We are a couple of blocks away."

Katelin said, "Well, I am taking you out for dinner, so stop at the front door to my office, and I will be right out. In fact, I can see you from my window."

Kate said, "I can see you. Dinner it is."

John opened up the sunroof and began waving back at Katelin. She was on about the 3rd floor of her building with a clear view of the boulevard.

Kate, Bill, and John got out of the car, and within 5 minutes, Katelin came running out with a big smile on her face and said, "I love you guys. I am so proud of what you have done."

All the windows by this time had people with the top part of their body leaning out and started applauding. Katelin hugged and kissed both of them together.

John and Kate waved to the people in the windows, and they let out a cheer. They then all got in the car. Katelin said, "OK, this is my treat, and I made reservations at our favorite restaurant, Deanne's Place. Both of you always say that when you eat there, it is like eating in heaven. The food and atmosphere are like you would expect in heaven."

John then with a proud look on his face said, "There are moments like this as a family we must always remember. I know that there are many moments in our lives, but this is one that is so good we must never forget it. I love both my girls."

Kate then said, "Let's always go to Deanne's Place if anything good or bad happens to us. Good to celebrate and bad to console each other."

Just then, the car pulled up to the restaurant. They all got out, and John said, "Bill can you join us?" Bill responded, "Thanks John, but I need to sit at a table between you and the door."

The restaurant was packed, and the waiter showed Kate, Katelin, and John to their table. As they sat down, everyone in the restaurant stood up and applauded. They had all seen the President's speech on television, and Katelin let the owner know this was a celebration dinner.

Anyway, both John and Kate were a little embarrassed since things like this always make them feel funny.

Katelin said, "You guys deserve it and gave them both a kiss again." John then said, "Let's eat. Food on the aircraft carrier was not that good."

Kate responded, "Yes, it has been a long day. I am starved."

The owner of the restaurant came over and said, "Dinner and drinks are on the house. Would you mind me taking a picture of the three of you? I will send you a copy."

Kate said, "OK, and thank you very much. This is our favorite restaurant."

John then turned to Katelin and said, "So how are you feeling? Anything exciting happening at work?"

"I am feeling great. The exciting thing happening at work is how everyone is coming up to me and telling me what great parents I have."

John said, "Katelin can you take off tomorrow? Your mom and I are thinking of doing some shopping and taking in a movie. Would you like to go?

"Thanks, Daddy, but since I have been out because of my illness, I better not miss any more days."

"We understand, but in two weeks, we are going to want you to come to the White House for a press conference."

"Just give me a time and date, and I will be there."

They all completed dinner at Deanne's and went home to relax.

RESTARTING THE MEDICAL PROJECT

For several days the President and Jim were making calls to countries that were not involved. The President also made a presentation to the United Nations in order to get them involved and enlist as many countries as possible.

Kate and John began making calls to the people that were involved in the project prior to the US stopping the project. All were being told that the United States was restarting the project and wanted to get them back into the picture. The same rules would apply in that the size of the country would govern the number of people that should be involved and the amount of money that they would contribute. The announcement to the world concerning the restart would be made in two weeks.

On the day of the press conference, they had every country in the world signed up. The President, Senate, and Congress leaders, Jim, Kate, and John, all met in the Oval Office to debrief the President on the status.

As soon as everyone was in the office, he told everyone, "Sit down. I have a little surprise for John." Just at that moment, Fabio, Caesar, Caesar's wife, Juan Carlos, the President of Brazil, Bill, Doris's parents, Katelin, and the US Ambassador to Brazil came to the oval office.

Jim, John, and Kate got up immediately and began hugging everyone. John stopped in front of Caesar's wife. Everyone was looking at John. He took her hands and said to Caesar's wife, "We found the people responsible for killing your son, and I want to give you your son's metal back. It did keep me safe. Thank you very much and gave her a hug and a kiss on her cheek."

Kate had a tear in her eye and also gave Caesar's wife a kiss and said, "Thank you for everything you have done. My husband really treasured the metal."

Doris's parents then came up to John and Kate. They were standing close together. Joe was a little nervous but looked at both John and Kate and said, "I want to thank both of you and also Jim and you, Mr. President, for getting the person responsible for my daughter's death. I know she will now rest in peace.

After everyone finished, the President said to everyone, "Please have a seat; the President of Brazil wants to present a metal to someone."

The President of Brazil then looked at John and said, "John, will you please come up here. I want to present this plaque and thank you for everything you have done for Brazil. This plaque is given to you for finding the people responsible for all the recent Medical Project killings and also for keeping our Medical Project on track.

John got up and said, "Thank you, Mr. President. I will share this honor with all the people in this room and also others that got the Medical Project back on track. Again, thank you from all of us."

The President of the United States then stood up and said, "Thank you all for coming. I believe we now have a press conference we need to go to. Shall we walk there together?"

The people that worked in the West Wing knew that there was going to be an announcement, so they surrounded the people that came out of the Oval Office, and when the President came out, they all applauded.

Everyone then walked together to the press room. As they were walking to the press conference, Jim advised the President that the room was packed with press from all over the world.

At the press conference, the President announced that Presidents and Leaders from all over the world would be making this same announcement. At that moment, with a big smile on the President's face, he said, "We are restarting Medical Project." Before he was able to get anything else out of his mouth, everyone at the press conference stood up and applauded. This does not usually happen at a press conference. They stood there applauding and cheering for a couple of minutes. You could almost hear and feel the same happiness around the world.

The President then said, "In a few weeks I will be calling another press conference with a new program I will be announcing and also some other projects we will be working on. The Congress, Senate and I need to come to some agreements before I make some more announcements. Think of it as the next book in a series of books with some of the same people with a few additional people added. For now, let's be very pleased that we are restarting the Medical Project with some of the best people in the world.

After the excitement of all the press conferences around the world, John, Kate, and the team were able to focus on making the Medical Project a success. After one year, all countries were using the information in the system, and you could measure a 50% reduction in death around the world.